A Time to Fly Free

A Time to Fly Free

Stephanie Tolan

Aladdin Books
Macmillan Publishing Company
New York

Collier Macmillan Canada
Toronto

Maxwell Macmillan International Publishing Group
New York   Oxford   Singapore   Sydney

First Aladdin Books edition 1990

Aladdin Books
Macmillan Publishing Company
866 Third Avenue
New York, NY 10022

Collier Macmillan Canada, Inc.
1200 Eglinton Avenue East
Suite 200
Don Mills, Ontario M3C 3N1

Printed in the United States of America
1 2 3 4 5 6 7 8 9 10

Library of Congress Cataloging-in-Publication Data
Tolan, Stephanie S.
   A time to fly free / Tolan.—1st Aladdin Books ed.
      p.   cm.
Summary: Ten-year-old Josh, who finds his private school
unbearable, joins forces with an elderly man in tending injured
birds.
   ISBN 0-689-71420-3
   [1. Birds—Fiction.] I. Title.
[PZ7.T5735Ti 1990]
[Fic]—dc20   90–31676 CIP AC

FOR RJ

May you always fly free.

A Time
to Fly Free

· 1 ·

THE BEATERS WERE CLOSING IN. Joshua Taylor had always thought his camouflage would keep him safe, but something had gone wrong. He could almost see them—natives circling a lion, shouting and pounding on gourds and pans, driving him inexorably toward the nets. He felt like that lion now, and he was almost in the nets. Almost.

He rested his cheek on one hand and winced. There must be a visible bruise by now, a clear symbol of what was happening. Outside the window, beyond the huge magnolia tree, the sun beat down on the Everett School's soccer field and seemed to vibrate the woods beyond. It was in the shade of that wood that he'd taken on his camouflage three years ago, in the first week of second grade. That day, like this one, had been a hot fall day, so muggy that even the breeze, with its faint odor of the Chesapeake Bay at low tide, had offered no real relief. During recess he had taken refuge from the heat in the woods, walking slowly through the shadows, where the still air seemed to hum with the lives of the creatures whose world it was. He had focused his eyes to see the smallest ones, the orb-weaving spider in the center of her web, the praying mantis swaying gently on a vine. Near the base of a tall, plate-barked pine he had discovered a butterfly, freshly emerged from its chrysalis. It was a tiger swallowtail, hanging from a branch of a low bush, just beginning to expand the wings that were still crumpled against its back. As Josh squatted to watch, the wings began ever so slowly to stretch with the rhythm of the fluid filling their minute veins. A ray of sunlight wavered across the butterfly as the leaves moved and sparked a flash of yellow in the darkness of one wing.

Behind Josh some of his classmates crashed through the weeds and in among the trees, Matthew Whittaker in the lead. "Hey!" Matthew yelled. "Whad'ya find this time? Another creepy-crawly?" One of the girls gave a high, pretend scream and the others giggled.

"A butterfly," Josh replied, his voice instinctively hushed, as if sound could disturb what was happening in front of him. "Watch."

"I don't see no butterfly," Matthew said, coming up next to Josh and nearly knocking him over. The others joined them, jostling each other for the best view.

Josh pointed. "There. It's just beginning to—"

"You mean that ugly thing?" Before Josh could answer, Matthew grabbed a stick and smashed the butterfly to the ground. It fell among the litter of twigs and brown pine needles, moved feebly, and then lay motionless, a dark, mangled bit of nothing. "Don't look like any butterfly to me. Come on, you guys! Last one to the big tree has to kiss Mrs. Eekin!"

Josh didn't move as the others tore off through the woods. He stared at what would have been the gold-and-black grace of the swallowtail, so casually and utterly destroyed. In spite of the heat, he shivered. His own life, the steady pulsing of blood in his veins, even the rise of goose bumps along the skin of his arms, seemed suddenly fragile. No one but Josh seemed aware of what had happened. No one but Josh had felt the chill or noticed the darkness that had come as swiftly as the stick in Matthew's hand. He picked up the crushed body and held it in his palm, breathing an apology to wings that would never fly.

When the bell rang to end recess that day, the Joshua Taylor who emerged from the woods and crossed the soccer field, the dead insect in one tightly closed hand, was a different Joshua Taylor. Like the fly that appears to be a hornet, the scarlet king snake that imitates the deadly coral snake, the viceroy butterfly that copies the dreadful-tasting monarch, Josh had decided to pretend to be what he was not. Like everyone else, he would ignore the lives in the woods and grass of the Everett School, because it was his interest in those lives that had brought death. From that day on, Josh would appear to be another Matthew Whittaker. As he walked into the classroom that day, Josh had dropped the butterfly's corpse into Mrs. Eekin's coffee cup. When she jumped and spilled the coffee down her dress later, the alliance between Josh and Matthew Whittaker had quietly begun.

Now Josh made an effort to focus on Ms. Daniels, his fifth-grade teacher, who was droning on at the front of the classroom. She was still talking about penmanship, neatness, and organization. He sighed and put his head down, resting his good cheek on his folded arms. The camouflage had not been easy to maintain at first, but as the months passed, it gradually became a habit. It was a little like putting on a clown suit every day as he waited for the school bus. He concentrated on humor, because it seemed the best way to keep his balance between the kids and the adults. He learned to refine the blunt wisecracks of Matthew's gang, making them funnier, coupling them with an innocent, ingratiating grin. He practiced the grin in front of his mirror, and it almost always worked, even with teachers who regularly sent the others to the office. Everybody liked Josh!

At recess, he was careful to do just what the other boys did, joining their mock battles, teasing the girls, roughhousing. It wasn't too bad, except when the gang went after Cole Simms. Cole was the smallest boy in their class, with arms and legs so thin they looked as if

4

they'd snap like dry twigs if he so much as fell down. Matthew taunted Cole about his size, about his nearly white blond hair, even about his enormous, pale blue eyes, magnified by the glasses he wore. Josh gritted his teeth when he joined the teasing, telling himself that he couldn't save Cole from it anyway. But Cole's pale, sad eyes came back to him, sometimes, in his dreams.

Still, the camouflage had worked. Matthew had accepted him, even made him second-in-command. In the second half of third grade, when they began to play soccer or football or baseball at recess and Josh discovered that his body was not a Matthew Whittaker body and couldn't pretend to be, he'd managed to work his fumbles into his clown act and keep the others laughing.

Until this year. Until the unaccountable changes that had begun with the start of the fifth grade. This year it was no longer funny when he missed the ball or kicked it the wrong way or tripped, because this year everybody wanted to win. There was no time for a clown on the soccer field. Matthew no longer chose him first, no longer chose him at all if he could help it. Then last week Matthew had pushed Josh off the bus, pretending it was an accident. And today, abandoning pretense, he had punched him first in the stomach and then in the face when Josh's mistake had let Johnny Staunton make a goal and Josh had tried to make a joke about it.

"Joshua!" The tone of Ms. Daniels's voice made it clear that this was not the first time she'd called his name. Josh raised his head and looked into those icy eyes. "What I've been saying should be of *particular* interest to you, Joshua. Perhaps you should get more sleep at home if you have such trouble staying awake in class." Josh kept his face carefully expressionless. "Have you finished reading your science chapter?"

He shook his head. He hadn't even begun the chapter that had been assigned on Monday. Today was Thursday, which meant the questions at the end of the chapter had to be answered in writing and turned in before science period tomorrow.

"You are in the fifth grade, Joshua Taylor. One could hope you would be able to finish a ten-page chapter in four days." Her eyes scanned the classroom. "How many of you have finished reading the chapter?"

Every hand went up. Josh didn't believe them all, but it didn't matter, he knew. Ms. Daniels didn't either. "You see? The rest of you may continue answering the questions. After we have discussed your answers tomorrow we'll do some microscope work." She looked back at Josh. "You will use the rest of today's period to finish the reading. The questions will be your homework, and I'll expect them to be handed in tomorrow with everyone else's. Written *neatly!*"

Josh took his science book out of his desk and stared at the Milky Way sprawled across its cover. That was only a trick—maybe to try to lure the *Star Wars/E.T.* generation into sampling science. There was only one chapter on astronomy in the whole book. If the trick worked, kids would get no more than a sampling of science, that was for sure. This six weeks the subject was biology. Six weeks to learn about "the science of life!" Six weeks! It would take that long to really learn about the living things he could scoop up in a collecting pan at low tide in front of the bulkhead at home.

It wasn't only that the kids had changed this year, he thought. It wasn't only that Ms. Daniels was different from the other teachers, hadn't even a shred of a sense of humor, and couldn't be melted even by the most perfect grin. Something about *himself* was changing. He felt like a crab when its old shell had cracked open and fallen away, leaving it soft and vulnerable until the new shell hardened. Or like a snake whose skin was too small but hadn't come off yet. Yes, that was it! A snake's eyes got cloudy, virtually blind, as the old skin began to detach itself. He was like that now—cramped and crowded and losing touch with the rest of the world. He'd always had a tendency to dream, to slip away when a teacher was talking, or when he was supposed to be working by himself at his desk. But he'd been able to keep himself focused when he *had* to, at least long enough to make passing grades. This year it was as if a soundproof wall went up whenever Ms. Daniels began to talk. No, that wasn't right. He could hear her voice. It was as if a scrambler had been built into his ears, turning words into meaningless noise. He would find himself looking out the window at the magnolia or the soccer field or the woods, thinking, remembering, dreaming. He didn't always know what had been happening in his mind when he'd be jolted back to the classroom, too late to catch up or cover up.

Josh turned to the chapter he was supposed to read. It began with scientific classification. The first paragraph compared classification to sorting buttons. Josh sighed. Sorting buttons. Imagine a biologist, trying to follow a single thread through the unimaginably complex web of life, thinking of his job as sorting buttons! Last year it would have seemed funny. Now it didn't. He forced himself to read on.

Suddenly he stopped and let his eyes travel back along the line he had been reading. There it was—the word "octopus," spelled out, in parentheses, as it was pronounced. Who needed to be told how to pronounce octopus? And if someone did need to be told how, what could that person hope to understand about biology, even from such a simpleminded book as this one? This was a fifth-grade class, as Ms. Daniels so often reminded him. How could a fifth grader *not* know how to pronounce octopus? How else could it be pronounced?

He looked around the room. The others were all busy at something, writing answers to the questions or

8

slumped in their seats with their books. No one else seemed to be bothered by the fact that the textbook people considered them imbeciles. They had been in school since they were five. Half their lives! And did people think so little had been accomplished in all those years that they wouldn't know by this time how to pronounce a word like *octopus*? Then why had they been forced to sit in those classrooms day after day?

Josh slammed his book shut as hard as he could. Chris Corbett, sitting next to him drawing fighter planes in his notebook, jumped, knocking his own science book to the floor.

Ms. Daniels looked up. Josh, his face feeling suddenly hot, crashed his fist down on his closed book and glared back at her. "Joshua Taylor," she said, "did you cause that disturbance deliberately?"

"Yes," Josh said.

"What? I didn't hear you."

"Yes! I said yes. I caused that disturbance deliberately!" Josh realized he was shouting. What was happening to him?

"I have had enough. You will report to Dr. Ellsworthy's office. Immediately."

Josh stood up. No one looked at him. Everyone seemed suddenly absorbed in the tops of their desks.

"*Now*, Joshua."

He walked down the aisle between the desks, feeling the eyes of the others on him now like lasers, raising blisters on his back.

· 2 ·

JOSH SAT ON THE BENCH outside Dr. Ellsworthy's office, wondering how he would explain the reason he'd been sent there. It wouldn't be so difficult if he were a straight A student. But A's on his report cards had been few and far between. Overall, he'd managed to maintain a C average, hardly a strong platform from which to condemn the school's choice of a science textbook. This year, of course, it was much worse. Failure was the promise in Ms. Daniels's eyes every time she looked at him.

A woman came out of Dr. Ellsworthy's office, followed by a man with a briefcase. They both glanced at Josh as they swept past him into the hall, and he felt like a specimen pinned to a display board. "Disruptive boy awaiting interview with headmaster" should be printed above his head. The secretary gave him what was probably intended as an encouraging smile. "You can go in now," she said.

Dr. Ellsworthy was standing behind his broad mahogany desk, his hands resting on the back of his leather swivel chair. "Well, Joshua, to what do I owe the honor of this visit?"

Josh decided to stick with the obvious. "Ms. Daniels sent me."

"Ahhh," Dr. Ellsworthy said, as if he were offering a wise and insightful comment on this revelation. He waved Josh to one of the chairs in front of his desk. "Sit down and let's see if we can get to the bottom of this." He spoke as if he had a particular "this" in mind, Josh thought. Ms. Daniels must have talked to him already. There was probably no hope of getting the man to see his side or to understand anything about what was happening to him this year. "Would you care to give me the particulars? Does it have anything to do with that—ah—wound beneath your eye?"

Josh touched his cheek. He'd forgotten the bruise. "No, sir. I don't think Ms. Daniels noticed that."

"Well?"

Josh wished Dr. Ellsworthy would sit down. He was a tall man, well over six feet, and built like a football player. To be sitting while he was standing made Josh feel like David facing Goliath.

"Well?" Dr. Ellsworthy repeated.

"I caused a disturbance in class," Josh said finally.

"Was this disturbance your usual—what shall I call it?—'verbal violence?' Or did you do something physical this time?"

"I guess you could say it was physical. I—um—hit my science book."

"Did you have a *reason* for this fistfight with a textbook? Or did you just want to make a noise?" Of course he had a reason—but not a reason he dared try to explain. "Are you having trouble with the work in the book, Joshua?"

"No, sir." *Not the way you mean trouble*, Josh thought.

Dr. Ellsworthy produced a long, dramatic sigh and went to a file cabinet near the window. Josh wondered if the man owned any suits that weren't gray or shirts that weren't white. His ruddy face stood out between his suits and his gray hair like a cardinal in a winter tree. Outside the window a mockingbird landed on a branch and jerked its tail crazily up and down. "Manic," Josh's mother called them. With a flash of white wing spots the bird flew away, and Josh looked back at the headmaster, who had dropped a folder in the center of his desk and was seating himself in his chair. He tapped the folder with one pink finger. "This is your file, Joshua. Do you know what it contains?"

It wasn't hard to guess. His report cards, with the twice-a-year comments from his past teachers about not working up to his potential. And their complaints about his poor work habits, his short attention span, his lack of interest in academic matters. There would be the results of the yearly achievement tests, too. He didn't know the exact results of those tests, but he figured they must be better than his grades or teachers wouldn't fuss about "potential" all the time. But did he really know what was in that folder? He shook his head.

"It contains disturbing evidence that you're not achieving here what you ought to achieve."

"Yes, sir." The idea was hardly a new one.

Dr. Ellsworthy frowned and leaned forward, clasping his massive hands on the folder. "As I'm sure you're aware, there has been a change this year, and that change is *more* than disturbing. Even though we haven't reached the end of the first grading period, Ms. Daniels has felt it necessary to enter a series of notes in your file. I've refrained from contacting your parents in the hope that what she has observed is no more than an unusually long readjustment period after summer vacation. But now here you are in my office, and I can't wait any longer. Ms. Daniels feels that you are being almost totally uncooperative this year."

Josh stared at the faded oriental carpet under the chair. The warp—or was it the woof?—showed through in one spot as if whole generations of children had sat here rubbing their feet nervously back and forth. He kept his own feet firmly on the rung of the chair.

"Can you give me any kind of explanation?" Josh

shook his head. "Ms. Daniels says that you have consistently failed to do the classwork she has assigned and have turned in only a small fraction of your homework. Is that the case?" Josh nodded. Dr. Ellsworthy's voice took on a note of sticky concern. Josh thought of the heavy sweetness of marshmallow creme. "Are you finding fifth-grade work to be more than you can handle, Josh?"

It all depended on what was meant by that, Josh thought. If he meant, as Ms. Daniels seemed to mean, was the work too hard to understand, then it was like telling him how to pronounce octopus—dumb. But in another way the work *was* more than he could handle: the interminable lectures on neatness and organization; the day-after-day sameness of copying the week's spelling words; the so-called discussions in reading class that led nowhere except to what had happened on page so-and-so; the ditto sheets of math problems. Actually, the truth probably was that everything about Ms. Daniels's fifth grade was more than he could handle.

"Look at me, son."

Josh tried to control the shudder that ran through him. He loathed people calling him "son." His father, the only man who could have the right to call him that, had died so long ago that Josh couldn't remember him. Even George, who by now might lay some claim to the word, didn't call Josh "son." He forced himself to look

14

into the eyes that were focused on him with suffocating concern.

"Sometimes a child, particularly an only child, gets a head start on other children in some areas. He's been around adults a lot, so he may read a little sooner, may use more difficult words. These things help on standardized tests, so he may get high scores in the first couple of years. But by fourth or fifth grade, things seem to collapse. The others catch up. It's as if a runner started a race out in front, running so fast that he can't sustain the pace. The other runners catch up and then pass him."

Josh felt his stomach tightening. He saw himself running down the soccer field while Matthew Whittaker breezed past him. Why did Ellsworthy have to compare schoolwork with athletics?

"But it's not too late, Josh. Ms. Daniels thinks that a little extra coaching—some after-school tutoring, actually—would help you catch up to your classmates."

Josh wanted to laugh. He wanted to be able to see this whole thing as funny. But it wasn't funny at all.

"What do you have to say, Joshua?"

"Nothing, sir." The only thing he could think of to say would probably be classified as "verbal violence."

"I'll be getting in touch with your parents, and we'll see what we can work out." Dr. Ellsworthy stood and came around the desk. When Josh got up, the principal put his arm around his shoulder and walked him toward the door. "We all get into a slump from time to time, but we mustn't give up." He gave Josh a pat on the behind. "Buck up, son. We'll get this problem taken care of and get you back in the game."

Josh went through the outer office and into the hall without looking back. He felt really sick to his stomach now. As he walked down the polished hall, he took slow, deep breaths, timing them with his steps. An after-school tutor! They wanted him to sit in a classroom all day, while the world went on without him outside, and then sit inside some more, with a tutor, who would give him more of the same stuff he'd been unable to force himself to do all day!

He reached the door of his classroom but didn't go in. He leaned against the bulletin board on the wall, where Ms. Daniels hung the work she considered good enough for display. On all the papers, the compositions and book reports, the spelling tests and math pages, in her precise red handwriting, were her favorite comments: "Neatly done" and "Careful work."

She would never post a paper of his on this board. What he *had* written this year had come back to him almost lost in a blizzard of red marks about his jagged, spiky handwriting, his spelling, his failure to follow the assignment or take it seriously. Never once the kinds of comments other teachers had always made—"creative approach" or "original thought." And certainly never the A's other teachers had given him on his writing.

Those had been the only A's he'd ever been sure of on schoolwork, and the only assignments he'd regularly enjoyed. Until this year, writing had been challenging —fun. He wondered what a tutor would "help" him write for Ms. Daniels. Something "careful," no doubt. And neat! And sure to follow the assignment exactly, no matter how dull!

It was almost time for the bell that would send students to the buses. Josh headed for the boys' rest room. He would not go back into that classroom today. He would not.

· 3 ·

Nᴵᴹᴮᵁˢ, his shaggy, white, part-sheepdog mutt, was barking as Josh unlocked the back door. By the time he was inside, she was jumping and wagging and licking the air in front of his face, too excited to sit still, but too well trained to put her paws on him. He slipped his backpack off, sat her down, and roughed up the fur that fell over her forehead and eyes. "Hi, girl. How was *your* day? Better than mine, I hope."

"Josh, is that you? Is it that late already?" Emily Forbes's voice came down from her second-floor studio. Josh went to the foot of the stairs, Nimbus trailing at his heels.

"It's four on the dot, Mom."

"Oh, Lord, and I'm not half finished with this!"

"You want to hear what I learned in school today?" It was their daily joke.

"Later, hon, okay? I've got this deadline. . . ."

"Okay. You wouldn't be interested in sorting buttons, anyway."

18

"Sorting what?"

"Never mind. Get back to work. I'm going to have something to eat and take Nimbus out." It was just as well, he thought. Sorting buttons might lead to his visit with Ellsworthy, and he didn't feel up to explaining to his mother about the tutor. He listened for a moment, as violin music swelled. His mother had turned the volume of her stereo up and gone back to her drawing board. Working as a free-lance illustrator, she always played classical music as she drew earrings and blouses for newspaper ads—to keep her at least partly sane, she said.

He could tell by the state of the kitchen, clearly untouched since breakfast, that it had been one of those days for her and she'd skipped lunch. When he got out the Oreos, he put several cookies and an apple on a plate, poured an extra glass of milk, and took the snack up to her studio. "Don't forget this," he warned her, setting it next to the stereo, "or the milk'll get warm."

"Ummm," she muttered. After a moment she glanced up, tossed her sandy hair over her shoulder, and smiled. "Thanks, Josh," she said, and bent over her work again.

Josh stood at the kitchen window as he ate his cookies and drank his milk, looking across the water of the river, its surface ruffled by an October breeze that had blown away the summerlike heat. Nimbus butted her head against the back of his legs until he gave her a handful of dog biscuits. "Tide's up," he said. "We have lots of time. Want to head over to the marsh?" Nimbus whined, her tail moving in sweeping circles. "Okay, let's go."

In the garage, he zipped his windbreaker, hung his binoculars around his neck, and picked up his oars, nets, and life vest. Nimbus frisked around his feet as he headed for the bulkhead at the end of his yard. "Will you stop that? It's hard enough to carry all this without you tripping me!"

His boat *Squeak*, short for *Pipsqueak*, was riding gently on the ripples, bumping against the piling she was tied to. He dropped his equipment into the boat, slipped his life vest on, then held the boat steady with one foot while Nimbus jumped in. She settled herself on the triangular molded seat that filled the point of the bow and waited, her tail circling steadily. Josh stepped in, fitted the oars into place, untied the line, and shoved off. Turning the bow toward the reeds across the river, he began to row, leaning into each stroke. He looked up into the deep blue of the sky overhead and felt his body begin to relax. As he rowed, the muscles in his arms tensed, bunched, relaxed, and tensed again, and all his other muscles seemed to let go. He'd been in the middle of the "fight-or-flight" syndrome most of the day, he thought. Adrenaline had been flowing, his whole body had been tensed, but there had been nothing to do with that energy, nowhere to run, no way to fight back. School was like a prison now, where even recess and gym, the supposed release periods, required watchfulness. Fellow prisoners could be as dangerous as guards.

"The great thing about animals," he said to Nimbus, behind him, "is that they never seem to waste energy worrying. If a cheetah starts to chase an antelope, the others in the herd run far enough to get out of the way, but as soon as they know it's somebody else being chased, they go right back to grazing again. Even the one who *is* being chased, if he manages to get away, just catches his breath and gets back to eating. It doesn't seem to occur to them that there might be a next time. No worrying. They either live or they die, and that's that. I wish I could be like that." Nimbus gave her usual answer, a thump of her tail against the seat.

A mullet jumped, silver against the blue sky, slapped back into the water, then jumped again. It was as if a small silver plate were being skipped across the river. Josh grinned. He loved the mullets. He liked to think they were laughing when they jumped, it was such a joyous leap and took them so high. They might be riding a roller coaster, out into the sun and back again. If *he* wanted to have an experience like that, he'd have to be able to leap out into space and back. Another mullet jumped. Fish clowns they were. Fish acrobats. Fish poets.

He stopped rowing and let *Squeak* drift with the

slight current. Sometimes he wanted to know *everything* about animals. But there were things he didn't want to know, too. If mullets only jumped to get away from predators, for instance, he didn't want to know that. It would take something away from that wild, joyous leaping. Of course, even if some scientist could prove they were only trying to avoid bigger fish, that scientist couldn't know how they *felt*. Surely even fish could feel something. What was it like to leap out of the murky world of the river and into the sun? Did they wish they could stay there, or were they glad to be down again, afterwards, in the comfortable darkness of the water? Did the sun dazzle them? Did they think the air world beautiful? Did animals have a concept of beauty?

He turned to look at Nimbus, who was staring intently toward the marsh. "Do you think it's a beautiful day?" he asked. She cocked her ears back at him but didn't take her eyes off the reeds. "You probably think beauty is a smell, anyway," he said. He imagined an art museum for dogs: nothing but smells. "Which would you like best, a steak being barbecued or a week-old dead fish?" An impatient thump of her tail reminded him he'd promised her the marsh. "Okay, okay."

As he turned back to the oars, he saw a great blue heron standing in the shallows at the edge of the reeds, gravely considering the water in front of it. Herons would never let the boat come nearer than fifty yards or so, no matter how slowly he moved, even when he didn't have Nimbus with him, even if he kept his face turned away. They would always let him come on for a while, as if they weren't even aware of his presence. Then they would raise their huge wings and flap unhurriedly off. They never seemed frightened so much as disdainful.

He raised his binoculars and gazed at the black-and-white head, its long crest plume lying flat against its neck. He wished he could tell it he meant no harm, that he only wanted to get to know it, one fellow creature to another. But he was stuck inside his human body—the ultimate threat. The heron kept its gaze on the water, purposely ignoring him, it seemed. Josh turned the boat slightly and began to row away. "No sense disturbing its dinner," he told Nimbus.

The marsh was his favorite spot—several acres of wilderness between the estates that sprawled along the river opposite the housing developments of Josh's own side. Among the reeds the mallards raised their young every spring and summer, safe from dogs and cats, hidden from the occasional fisherman or crabber who might come near. And here herons and egrets hunted, here he could watch the muskrats and the water snakes, the fiddler crabs whose holes dotted the mud-banks and the blue crabs feeding in the shallows. In two huge trees behind the marsh the egrets roosted in late summer, flying in at dusk and talking loudly among themselves before settling for the night. From Josh's backyard, the distant trees looked like fruit trees at harvest time, heavily loaded with huge, white fruit. But when he came close in *Squeak*, the trees came alive with the movement of wings and the sound of egret voices. He always thought they were telling each other what kind of a fishing day it had been, gossiping and comparing notes.

When he judged himself far enough away from the heron, Josh edged in among the reeds, sending clouds of gnats and midges into the air. He'd be glad when the autumn chill demolished the gnat population. They seemed to be among the last to desert the marsh, and they bit much harder than their size would lead anyone to expect. Nimbus shook her head and then seemed to ignore the insects, only occasionally blinking when they landed on her eyelids. Josh took out the insect repellent he kept in his jacket pocket and rubbed the white lotion on his neck and face and then on his hair.

A yellow styrofoam tray that had held chicken was caught at the base of a reed hummock, its plastic wrap trailing in the gentle movement of the water. Except that it was slightly sun-faded and edged with green algae, it could have been dropped yesterday. Josh could still read the label stuck to the plastic wrap. It was a relic of the crabbing season, had probably been in the water for a month. Did the crabbers think it would just go away if they dropped it? He didn't mind their catching crabs. There weren't any professional crabbers around here, and no one caught very many. But he minded their tossing their trash into the river as if it were a garbage can. He scooped up the tray in his seining net and dumped it on the bottom of the boat. Now that autumn was here, he wouldn't be using his nets for catching creatures much anymore. Life was preparing for winter, burrowing into the mud, heading for deeper water, flying south. Eventually the marsh would seem to be a dead place, visited only by gulls and a few ducks.

The heron flew over them and landed high in a twisted field pine. Josh could almost feel the breeze from its huge wings. It wouldn't migrate, he thought. But he wouldn't see much of it, either. He didn't know where herons spent their time in the winter. Light from the lowering sun tinged bird and tree with gold. "I love it here," Josh said to Nimbus. "Just now, just here, just the way it is this minute." But winter was coming, as surely as tomorrow was coming, and school and Ms. Daniels and Dr. Ellsworthy. Josh wished for wings. He longed for the freedom to migrate, to escape the winter prison and join the birds somewhere in the sun. It would be strange and new, the place where the sun was, and maybe he wouldn't mind so much being an alien there. It would be better than being an alien here, in a world that was supposed to be home.

· 4 ·

FRIDAY WAS CLOUDY, with a damp chill that pre-saged winter in spite of the red-gold of the sweet gum leaves and the still-green grass. Many of the seed pods of the magnolia had split, and shiny red seeds were beginning to show. From Josh's desk, the seed pods looked as if they were covered with soft red velvet. When he'd come inside that morning, he'd noticed one flower at the very top of the tree. He couldn't see it now, but it seemed sad somehow to know it was there —the last one, beginning to droop, the huge, creamy petals unable to support their weight. They would fall soon, and the tree would go into its own kind of hibernation. It would pull back into itself, only its roots growing through the long nights and cold winter days. It was odd, Josh thought, that some evergreens managed to survive winter without having evolved the pine's advantage, the leaves like needles. Evergreens. Ms. Daniels should like evergreens. Neat trees. No disorganized changing of colors, no litter of leaves all over the ground.

". . . You can't tell by just looking at the problem how many times 85 might go into 3,264. So you break it down and began with the divisor's first digit. . . ." Ms. Daniels was explaining long division again. She had put a different problem on the board, of course, but the explanation today was the same one she had given yesterday, the same as the day before. Of all the boring subjects they'd thought up to teach children, nothing, Josh thought, could be more boring than long division. The idea of it was simple enough, but all that awful repetition! And all that writing! Each problem took up half a page and a ridiculous amount of time. All Josh could think of, as he looked at the board, was how fast his calculator could give the answer—as fast as he could punch its buttons. No matter how many long division problems they did, no matter how fast they got, none of the kids in this room would ever be able to compete with a five-dollar calculator. Anyway, how many of them would ever have to do long division once they'd left the Everett School? Unless their calculator batteries went dead. And if that happened, just at the moment there was a desperate need to do a problem in long division, every one of them could manage to struggle through it. Then they would rush to a drugstore for a battery.

Josh imagined a stooped figure wearing wire-rimmed glasses, a fingerless glove on the hand that clutched a quill pen. He was perched on a high stool, bending over gigantic ledger books. Bob Cratchit, doing the figures for Ebeneezer Scrooge's business. But there weren't any Bob Cratchits anymore. Even adding machines had been replaced by calculators and computers. There would never be a Bob Cratchit again, unless a nuclear war dumped the whole country back into the Stone Age. And if that happened, there would be a lot more pressing problems than long division to worry about! Making American children practice long division was about as worthy a use of their time, he decided, as making them practice smoke signals in case the telephone systems quit. Or teaching them to cook over open fires. Surely the calculator was as much a part of life today as the stove. The Everett School had bought two computers for the junior high, but here in the fifth grade was Ms. Daniels, going on as if the silicon chip had never been invented.

Josh ran the tip of his pencil along the groove in his desk, darkening the line at the bottom, watching the fine graphite powder appear like soot behind the moving point.

"Joshua, would you care to answer that?"

Josh looked up. He had done it again. He hadn't heard the question, of course. "Could you repeat the question please, ma'am?" Out of habit, Josh put on his most winning smile.

"I suggest that a student who didn't finish half the problems on the pretest and made several errors in the problems he *did* finish might find paying attention helpful." Josh continued to smile, his cheeks stiffening with the effort. "I asked what the nine tells us in this problem." She pointed to the board: 5,634 divided by 79.

"I'm sorry, ma'am, it isn't talking loud enough for me to hear." A demon seemed to have taken over his tongue.

In the breathless silence that greeted his words, the look in Ms. Daniels's eyes became deadly. She shook her head. "Nothing gets through to you, does it, Joshua?" She tapped her chalk against the chalk tray. "Since you don't see the need to listen to an explanation, you may spend the rest of the math period completing a problem sheet. Maybe that will give you something worthwhile to focus on."

She watched, still tapping her chalk, while he got up and went to the box of dittoed problem sheets on the windowsill in the front of the room. As he returned to his seat, carefully stepping over the foot Chris Corbett stuck out across the aisle, she turned away. "Jessica, would you please answer the question for us?"

Josh sat down and placed the dittoed sheet on his desk, lining it up so that it was the same distance from all four edges. He picked up his pencil and bit the last of the eraser off the end, testing its resiliency against his back teeth. Ms. Daniels's voice continued to buzz around his ears like a mosquito. "Exactly. So we can think of the 79 as 80 instead. What shall we put down, then? David?"

Josh looked at the ten hazy purple problems on the sheet in front of him. Ms. Daniels had said "something *worthwhile*." How did she know what went on inside his head and whether it was worthwhile or not? At dinner last night, his mother and George had been talking about strip mining and marsh draining, about air pollution and water pollution and the purposeful killing of wildlife. In a world where all that was happening, did Ms. Daniels really believe that long division was worthwhile? In a world on the very edge of a nuclear holocaust, could this dittoed math sheet be considered worthwhile? Even as a joke? His stomach was clenching up again, as it had in Dr. Ellsworthy's office. The beaters were nearly on him now, banging their noisemakers in his ears. And the net was right there. He was almost in it.

"Joshua!" He didn't look up. He heard her footsteps and the repetition of his name. "Joshua Taylor!" She was next to him now. If he glanced sideways, he would see her skirt, but he kept his eyes on the page in front of him. A hand holding a piece of chalk entered his field of vision and banged that chalk on a problem in the middle of the page. "I expect you to do these problems now, Joshua. Right now."

There was no explaining what happened to him. It was almost as if her chalk had come down on a detonator, as if a bomb had gone off, catapulting him to his feet and knocking his chair into the desk behind him. He was aware of Ms. Daniels backing away, but he didn't look at her. He didn't look anywhere but straight ahead, as some force other than his own mind seemed to be moving him down the aisle to the front of the room. Next to the door, he stopped long enough to take his jacket and empty backpack off their hook; then he opened the door and went out.

He put his jacket on as he walked, his footsteps echoing in the empty hall. He could hear Ms. Daniels calling his name, but he didn't stop. Then he was through the double entrance doors and outside. He slipped his arms into the straps of his backpack and began to run down the long driveway the buses came up every day, past the flagpole and on past the brick gates with their brass plaque saying "The Everett School, Founded 1923."

When he reached the street, Josh slowed to a walk. He had no money with him, not even enough for a phone call. Anyway, if he called his mother, what would he say? That he was sick? If he told her about the stomachache, about yesterday's stomachache, she might take him to the doctor and they'd find out there was nothing wrong with him. At least nothing a doctor could fix.

Could he tell her the truth? What was the truth? Could he explain—to his mother or anyone else— about native beaters? Would anyone understand that he was like something wild, something that would be destroyed forever if the nets were allowed to close around him? It was a matter of survival—of life and death. He would have to find a way to tell her, to tell George, that if they made him go back to the Everett School again they would ruin him the way a lion was ruined when he was locked in a cage and left to pace back and forth along the bars.

As he thought that, it seemed as if the sun had come out, as if he had scraped off his too-tight skin and his eyes were clear again. He looked up and saw that the heavy clouds were still there, moving slowly on invisible winds. But the sense of sunlight stayed with him. He was free! He had walked out the door and no one had stopped him. He was actually free!

· 5 ·

TWO HOURS LATER, Josh was feeling less free than tired and hungry. Walking home had to be *possible*, he reasoned. But however possible, it was anything but easy. He'd ridden the bus to school since kindergarten and he knew the route perfectly well. But a large part of that route was on a highway where pedestrians weren't allowed. The only other road that went reasonably straight in the right direction went through commercial areas the whole way, areas full of shopping plazas and grocery stores, car dealers and banks, MacDonald'ses and gas stations. It was designed for cars. There were no sidewalks, no crosswalks or walk lights. The road itself was full of trucks and buses and cars going too fast between traffic lights. He had begun to feel very small and vulnerable.

He had also begun to feel incredibly conspicuous. It had never occurred to him before that between the hours of nine and three, five days a week, the world was a world devoid of children. It was as if he'd been dropped behind enemy lines in full uniform. There was no camouflage that could make a ten-year-old look as if he belonged here. If he wasn't blown off the edge of the road by a semi or suffocated in bus exhaust, he'd probably be arrested for truancy.

So he had taken refuge in the smaller streets of the residential areas. Here there were sidewalks. Here there was hardly any traffic. But here, also, the streets curved and wandered and ended suddenly in cul-de-sacs against the water. Josh had never fully appreciated the significance of calling this part of Virginia "the Tidewater." Suddenly it seemed that there was more water than land. The rivers had whole networks of creeks and the creeks had branches—even the branches had branches. Only the really major streets had bridges. The others just ended. Time and again, just when he was sure he was going the right direction and beginning to make good time, he'd have to stop and either follow a street that went all the way around one of the smaller inlets, or retrace his steps and look for a street important enough to offer a bridge.

It was after one o'clock. If he went on like this, at least he wouldn't have to explain getting home early. In fact, if he got any more confused than he was now, he might have to explain being late instead. He stopped again. Ahead of him this street, too, ended in a cul-de-sac, the houses angled around the circle on pie-shaped yards, loblolly pines towering over them. Between two houses he could see the gray sky reflected metallically on water. Josh swallowed hard. The prickling sensation behind his eyes would give way to tears if he let it. What he most wanted to do was to sit down where he was and just give up. Someone might come along in a car and offer to drive him home. Or some Good Samaritan might come out of one of the houses to ask what he was doing there. Maybe he should just go up to a house and ask to use the phone. His mother would come pick him up. He didn't really have to spend the rest of his life wandering up and down these curving streets like Theseus in search of the Minotaur.

But with the thought of home came the thought of his mother and the questions she would ask. They were questions he wasn't ready to answer. He didn't know, yet, what he could say. In the last two hours he had felt younger and younger and younger. Ten. A fifth grader. Since when could a ten-year-old decide to walk out of school and never go back? He couldn't even find his way home. What had he been thinking of? No, he couldn't call home. He'd created this mess for himself, and he had to get out of it by himself. How could he expect them to listen to him otherwise?

He looked at the water glinting between the two houses at the far end of the cul-de-sac. Why should water be an enemy all of a sudden? It was *his* water, after all. Somewhere it connected with the river he'd been out on yesterday. Maybe he was close enough to home by now to be able to recognize something. Maybe he'd explored whatever creek or inlet this was in *Squeak* sometime. Maybe if he saw the houses from the water side, he would at least know where he was.

There didn't seem to be any sign of life in either of the two houses. One was a brick ranch house with all its curtains pulled, its door and storm door looking firmly shut, its carefully clipped hedges like a barrier between itself and the street. The other was a rambling, wood-sided house, stained dark brown. The stain had weathered unevenly, giving the house an unbalanced look, and the white trim was peeling. The windows had no curtains but were covered instead by something that looked like strings and beads. The front door, unprotected by a storm door, was carved wood and looked older than the house itself. It was cracked and weathered to the shade of old driftwood. The shrubs in front of this house were overgrown, the lawn patchy and uncut.

Between the houses, growing against a cyclone fence, a tall hedge stretched back toward the water. Josh walked along next to the hedge, staying in the yard of the brick house. If anyone did happen to be there, the curtains would keep them from seeing him. The yard ended in a concrete bulkhead bordered by more bushes. It looked as if they were tall enough to cut off entirely the view of the creek from the windows of the house. Josh wondered why anyone would live in a house on the water without being able to see it. Across the creek were other ranch houses, their back yards also ending in bulkheads, some concrete, some wood, some carefully tended, others sagging or crumbling. Josh realized sadly that he didn't recognize anything after all. It could be any of a hundred creeks. The only thing noticeable about it was that it seemed to be deeper than some. It was only a couple of hours past dead low tide, and there were no mud flats to be seen.

Josh sighed. The only thing to do was go back to the major street and take his chances with the buses and trucks. This was getting him nowhere. Just as he turned to go back, a piercing shriek froze him. It had come from the other side of the hedge. For an instant he envisioned an axe murder, and then the shriek was repeated. He laughed. How could he have mistaken a sea gull for a person? A third shriek was followed by the "har-har-har-har" of a laughing gull. He found a break in the hedge and peered through. As if he were looking through his binoculars, he found himself staring at the head of a great blue heron. The eye was very bright, very alert under the black cap and seemed to be staring back at him. It was very close. The bird could be no more than a foot from the fence on the other side of the hedge. The cry of the gull came again and the heron turned its head slowly, tilting it slightly, apparently looking down at the gull Josh couldn't see.

Josh glanced back at the brick house, at its windows like closed eyes. Then he balanced himself on the concrete bulkhead, took hold of the post at the end of the fence, and swung himself out over the water and around to the other side. He was so startled by what he saw that he almost went backwards into the water. Standing in the sparse grass of the yard was the heron, one wing held firmly to its body with an elastic bandage. Near its feet, stabbing peevishly at a partial loaf of dried bread, was the sea gull, its wings spread slightly to give it balance. It was standing on one gull leg and a kind of peg leg made of wood and held in place by a harness of nylon webbing. Josh could hardly have been more surprised to see it wearing a tiny eye patch and gold earring. The gull shrieked irritably, and the heron took one long, sedate step away. It looked at Josh, blinked, pulled in its long neck to rest its head on its shoulders, and seemed to go off into a meditative trance. Both birds were behind a low fence that enclosed a part of the yard. Against the hedge in their pen was a kind of lean-to, a rough wooden shelter. In another, smaller pen, there were two box turtles and a pan of browning apple wedges.

"Get out! Get out! Beware of the dog!" The voice was deep and loud, and Josh jumped guiltily. He looked around but could see no one. "Get out! Get out! Hello!" A movement caught his eye. Near the back porch of the house, in the lowest branch of a

38

dogwood tree, almost hidden among the scarlet leaves, was a huge, black crow. "Bad dog," it said. "Hello."

"Hello," Josh said. He took a few steps forward, glancing around for the dog. He didn't see one. "Is there really a dog?"

The crow raised its wings. "Awwk! Get out!" it screamed. "Beware!"

Josh still saw no dog. The bulkhead on this side of the fence was made of wood, and a ramshackle dock stretched into the water, tilted slightly as if settling into the mud on one side. A battered aluminum johnboat was tied to the dock. A group of mallards clustered nervously near the dock, muttering to each other and watching him. If there were a dangerous dog around, surely they wouldn't be staying there like that. Josh moved closer to the crow. "It's okay, fella," he said. "I won't hurt you." He had heard about tame crows, knew they could be taught to speak. But he'd never seen one before and hadn't realized they were so big or that their voices could be so human. It didn't sound anything at all like a parrot. The crow raised its wings again as Josh came closer, and Josh saw that the toes on one of its feet were nothing more than blunt knobs. It held to its perch with its good foot only. "What happened to your toes?" Josh asked.

"Get out!" the crow replied. It folded its wings and cocked its head at him, still wary. "Out, out, out," it muttered.

Josh grinned. He'd asked a question as if the bird could answer him. The human voice had made him forget it was only mimicking and didn't understand the words it used. He looked around again. Still no sign of a dog. The mallards had settled down now, a few of them sinking to the ground and tucking their bills under their wings. Josh saw that what he'd taken for a porch at first glance was not really a porch. It had a roof and one painted plywood side, but it was really a bank of cages of different sizes, built of wood and heavy wire mesh. Inside several of them were birds. Keeping an eye on the crow, Josh walked over to the cages. In one was a kingfisher with two good wings and two good legs but only one eye. In another was a female mallard, busily preening her feathers. Josh could see nothing wrong with her. In another was a huge herring gull, standing very still and regarding Josh coldly. The look reminded Josh of Ms. Daniels and he laughed. Behind him, the crow mimicked his laugh, subsiding into a series of low chuckles. "What's the problem with *you*?" Josh asked the gull.

Suddenly, with a tremendous, cawing shout, the crow launched itself off its branch. With a rush of wings, it flew over Josh's head. "Hey, kid!" a voice said. "What're you doing there? Get out!"

"Get out, get out," the crow repeated in an identical voice. A man was standing at the corner of the house, the crow on his shoulder. He was wearing a faded flannel shirt, green work pants, worn and stained, and leather boots with thick, orange soles. Long, gray hair stuck out beneath an old baseball cap and his face was sunburned and heavily lined.

"I said, get out of here. You've got no business in my yard messing with my birds."

"I wasn't messing—" Josh began.

But the man cut him off, taking a step toward him and raising his fist. "Get out now, the way you got in, or I call the cops!"

"Beware of the dog!" the crow screamed, fidgeting excitedly on the man's shoulder. "Bad dog! Get out!"

"Yes, sir," Josh said, and backed toward the bulkhead, his heart pounding. The ducks, having stood up and begun waddling toward the old man, retreated again, quacking vociferously.

"If I ever catch you in this yard again, you'll be sorry!"

Josh turned and fled, swinging himself around the fence. "Rafferty," he heard the crow say, his voice higher than before. "Rafferty, Rafferty!" The words were followed by a long string of what must have been crow language. Josh ran halfway along the hedge and then crouched to get his breath. He felt as if he'd run a block. He could hear the man on the other side of the fence now, speaking in low, comforting tones. Josh couldn't make out words, but he seemed to be talking to the birds. And the birds responded. Soft, steady quackings and chuckling noises blended with the man's voice.

Josh looked at the brick house. Still no sign of life. He knew he should go. What if the guy did call the cops? Wasn't there enough to explain when he got home as it was? *If* he got home. But he stayed very still, listening to see if the man would come to be sure he'd really gone. The low voice went on, and now he heard the sound of water filling a metal bucket. He remembered a washtub in the pen with the heron and sea gull. However ferocious the old man had been with him, he certainly seemed gentle enough with the birds. The crow had seemed as happy to see him as Nimbus was when Josh got home. "Rafferty," the crow had said. Was that the man's name or the crow's? And was the guy a vet? Surely he was responsible for the bandages and the strange, hand-fashioned peg leg the laughing gull wore.

Josh's knees began to cramp from the squatting position he was in. Slowly, as quietly as possible, he lowered himself to the ground and peered between the branches. The leaves were too thick here for him to see clearly, but he could still hear the water running. Every so often the crow said a few of his human words, his voice changing from time to time.

The breeze off the river seemed colder now, pushing insistently down Josh's jacket collar and ruffling his hair. The clouds were lower and darker. Suddenly Josh was overwhelmed with exhaustion. He wrapped his arms around his legs and rested his chin on his knees. Again the urge to cry swept over him, but he forced it back. He would just sit here for a little and rest. Then he would get up and go home, in spite of the buses and the trucks and being the only child loose in the world. But right now he would rest. Just for a little while. He leaned gingerly against the springy, prickly hedge. Just for a few minutes.

· 6 ·

A COLD SPLASH on his nose startled Josh. Another landed on his head. He blinked. Had he fallen asleep? It didn't seem possible, but maybe he had. He pushed himself to his feet, feeling stiff all over. It was nearly two according to his watch; he'd have to get going. And now he'd be soaked long before he could get home. The drops of rain were large and intermittent, but it looked as if a steady downpour would arrive any minute. A bank of dark, fast-moving clouds was advancing toward the creek, and he'd have to head straight into the worst of it to get home.

He looked through the hedge again but couldn't see the man, or hear him. Had he gone inside? What Josh wanted more than anything, more, even, than getting home dry and safe, was to go back to that yard again. He wanted the crow to talk to him again. He wanted to know what was wrong with the duck and the gull in those cages and what had happened to the heron's wing, the laughing gull's leg.

44

It began to rain harder, the drops not so big now, but constant. Josh hunched his shoulders but didn't move. He was going to get wet anyway, so there was no point in worrying about it. Surely, with the rain, the man would stay inside his house. Maybe it would be possible to go back—just for a few minutes. He squinted through the hedge. It was as if the yard were a magnet and Josh a pile of iron filings. Slowly, taking a step and then stopping to listen, he crept back down the bulkhead. He imagined himself a terrorist, sneaking into a nuclear power station. Of course he didn't need to cut the fence and crawl through. All he had to do was swing around the end again. He stood for a moment, one hand on the fence post. No sound except the rain. What would the old guy really do if he caught him there again? He wouldn't shoot him or anything, would he? And if he called the police, as he'd threatened, what would happen then? Maybe they wouldn't even come. And if they did, he was only ten after all. What would they do to a ten-year-old for trespassing except give him a lecture and maybe take him home and talk to his mother? Heck with it, Josh thought. It's worth the chance!

He swung out and around, half expecting to see the old man waiting for him with a shotgun. But the yard contained only the birds. The wild mallards, oblivious to the rain, were asleep in clusters against the bulkhead. The heron had taken refuge in the lean-to, while the gull stood outside, looking almost comically miserable, though he was partly sheltered by the leaves of the oak tree that grew just outside the pen.

Josh couldn't see the crow. The branch it had stood on before was empty. It had probably gone inside with the man, he thought, disappointed. There were no lights on in the house, in spite of the steadily darkening sky. Maybe the man had gone entirely! He moved closer to the dogwood.

"Hello!" The voice was as startling as a gunshot. Josh felt as if his heart had stopped. "Beware of the dog, dog, dog." In the upper branches of the tree a wooden box had been nailed on its side. The crow was standing on a perch inside the box, looking at him.

Josh swallowed and grinned up at the bird. "I'm glad that's you. Would you come out? The rain isn't that bad."

The crow regarded him steadily, as if considering his request. Then, to Josh's surprise, he stepped out, hesitated a moment, and flew down to the lower branch, only slightly above Josh's head. "Hello, bad dog," it said companionably.

"Hello, crow. I'm not a dog, you know. I'm a boy. You crow, me boy. Got that? I'm *not* a dog."

"Dog, dog, dog," the crow answered.

"Stubborn, aren't you? Do you bite? Would you come on my arm?" He held his arm up toward the bird, gritting his teeth as he did it, hoping the bird didn't bite. The closer he got to it, the bigger it looked, and the more dangerous its beak. He almost hoped it wouldn't take him up on his invitation.

The crow cocked its head, looking at his arm. Holding his breath, Josh raised the arm a little, moving it very slowly closer, until it nearly touched the bird's breast. Gravely, the crow raised its wings slightly and hopped on, its good foot gripping with powerful claws. Josh kept his arm out, away from his face, feeling his heart quicken with excitement. The crow had actually come to him! "Do you have a name?" he asked it. "What's your name?"

"His name is Grock."

Josh jumped, the crow squawked, waving its wings and gripping even more tightly, its claws biting through his jacket and into his arm. Josh forced himself to stand still, turning only his head to avoid the wings. The man was standing beside the cages. Josh had been so intent on the crow, he hadn't heard him coming. At least there was no gun. Josh cleared his throat, but even so, his voice came out sounding choked. "If he's Grock, are you Rafferty—sir?"

"It's raining," the man said.

"Yes, sir."

"You're some gutsy kid, coming back here after I told you to get out."

Josh didn't answer. He didn't feel gutsy. His arm

was shaking. The crow fluffed its feathers and muttered a long stream of crow language.

"It's two o'clock," the man said. "On a Friday. You got anything to say about that?"

"No, sir."

"That's what I figured." They stood for a moment, staring at each other. Josh made an effort to keep from looking away, and it was the old man who broke first, looking instead at the crow. Gradually his face changed. He didn't smile, but his expression softened. "To answer your question, kid, yes. I'm Rafferty. You want to tell me who you are?"

"Joshua Taylor." The crow pecked at Josh's watch.

"Better switch arms," Rafferty said. "Grock likes watches. If he can't get it off, he's liable to get mad. That wouldn't do your watch any good."

Josh moved his other arm slowly toward the crow and pushed it against its breast. Grock, after another peck at the watch, jumped onto Josh's other arm. "What happened to his foot?"

"I don't know. I found him with his toes all cut up. Maybe a trap. Sometimes I know what happened, sometimes not. I don't always like knowing." Rafferty looked up at the sky. "I don't know how *you* feel about rain, but I don't get my kicks standing around getting drenched. I'm going in." He walked past Josh and up two concrete steps to the back door, then he turned around. "You coming?"

"Uh—I—actually, I'd better be getting home."

48

"I didn't notice much of a rush to do that before. I'm not dangerous. It's okay."

"It isn't that. . . ."

"Get off, Grock," Rafferty said. "Just give your arm a little toss and he'll go back to his box. He isn't crazy about rain either, but I don't let him in the house."

Josh did as he was told. "Beware of the dog," the crow said and flew up to his box, as Rafferty had said he would.

"So come in," Rafferty said, as he opened the door. "You passed the test."

"What test?"

"Grock doesn't go to people. Except me. And you, apparently. Now come in and get out of the wet."

Josh went past the man into a kitchen, wiping his feet on a rag rug inside the door. Rafferty followed, also wiping his feet, and went directly across the room to the refrigerator. He opened the door and turned back to Josh. "You hungry?"

Josh started to say no, to be polite, but his stomach growled, and he nodded his head.

"I figured as much. Take off that wet jacket and sit down." He waved toward an oak table in the middle of the faded linoleum floor. Two different chairs, both with carved backs, faced each other across the table. Josh slipped off his backpack and jacket and stood holding them awkwardly. "Just hang 'em on the back of the chair."

Rafferty took a beer out of the refrigerator and set it

49

on the table. Then he took out a loaf of wheat bread, a chunk of cheddar cheese, and a carton of milk. "Cheese sandwich okay? It's what I've got."

"Sure." Josh sat down.

"How about honey? Ever had cheese and honey?"

"No, sir."

"Try it." He took a jar of honey out of a cabinet beside the refrigerator and put it next to the cheese. Then he got out a plate, a knife, a cheese slicer, and two glasses, and settled himself in the other chair. "Go ahead and fix yourself a sandwich. Spread honey on the bread and put the cheese on top. It's good!" He filled one of the glasses with milk and pushed it across to Josh, then poured the beer into the other. "You don't live around here." He leaned back until his chair was balanced on its back legs.

"No, sir." Josh dipped the knife into the honey jar and dripped honey on the table. "Sorry."

Rafferty took a dishcloth off the edge of the sink and tossed it to him. "So, you lost?"

Josh wiped up the honey before answering. "Not exactly," he hedged. "If I had my boat. . . ."

"What kind of boat?"

"Just a little fiber glass dinghy."

"Motor?"

"No. It's really small. I just row."

"And you could get home by boat, but not on foot."

"It's harder walking." Josh finished making the sandwich and took a bite. Rafferty was right. Cheese and honey *was* good. "What's the matter with the herring gull?"

"Infection. He's nearly well."

"Are you a vet?"

Rafferty laughed. "If you mean veterinarian, no. How'd you know it was a herring gull?"

"I just know. *Larus argentatus* is its scientific name. It means 'silvery gull.' "

"You know any others? How about the heron?"

Josh swallowed and took a sip of milk, trying to remember. He'd known all the common ones once. "*Ardea herodius*. And the other gull—with the peg leg—that's *Larus atricilla*, the laughing gull. The mallards are *Avas platyrhynchos*."

"You know Grock's?"

"No, sir. Sorry."

"How about the turtles?"

"No. I just learned the birds I see all the time—the egrets and gulls and ducks."

"Did you learn all this in school?"

Josh took as big a bite of the sandwich as he could and stared down at the wood grain of the tabletop. When he'd finally finished chewing, he shook his head. "Not in school. No, sir."

"I didn't think schools had changed that much." He finished his beer and plunked the glass onto the table, letting his chair fall back to all four legs. "Do me a favor, will you, kid?"

"Yes, sir."

"Quit calling me sir. The name is Rafferty. Not Mr. Rafferty, just Rafferty. And never, *never* sir! I hate phony respect. If I deserve your respect, I guess I'll get it, and if you deserve mine, you'll get that. If you don't, you'll know it. Okay?" Josh nodded. "Good." Rafferty leaned back again and watched while Josh finished the sandwich and milk.

Josh, embarrassed at being watched as he ate, looked around the kitchen. It was clean but looked like the house from the front—run down. The counters were stained, the cupboards worn around the handles, the pattern on the floor faded. Josh finished his milk. "Why does Grock talk about a dog? Do you have a dog?"

Rafferty looked away, his face still and unreadable. For a long time he said nothing. Finally, he shook his head. "Used to. Big, old, scary-looking Doberman, she was. Named Schnitzel. She died in August. Twelve years old." He sat upright again. "Dogs ought to live longer!"

"Did Grock like her? He says 'bad dog' all the time."

Rafferty laughed. "I used to call her that, like a nickname, trying to give her a little more sense of what she was supposed to be. You know, big Doberman watchdog type. She was nothing but a softie! That's why I taught Grock to say, 'Beware of the dog.' She needed all the help she could get. That crow used to drive her crazy, riding on her shoulder, biting her ears. They had kind of an understanding, though, I guess. One weird crow and one weird Doberman. Listen, I've got a couple more errands to run and it's still raining out there. You want a ride home?"

Josh grinned. "Sure! Thanks." Maybe it was that he wasn't hungry anymore. Or maybe it was that Rafferty hadn't asked him why he wasn't in school, or that Grock had come onto his arm. But for some reason, he felt great again, and the thought of the questions his mother would ask wasn't so terrible. He'd think of some way to answer them.

Rafferty's vehicle was like his kitchen, his dock, his bulkhead, his house. It was an old pickup truck with battered fenders, its tailgate held up with twisted wire. Its blue was faded and spotted with rust. Inside, the seats were patched with tape and the motor filled the cab with labored grinding until it finally started with a cough. Once started, though, it ran smoothly. Josh suspected that however Rafferty's belongings might look on the outside, they were probably dependable.

"Where to?" Rafferty asked as they pulled out of the driveway. "I hope it's not far from the lumberyard. This is no taxi." Josh gave him the address. "You weren't all that far by boat—maybe half an hour rowing. Hell of a walk, though."

Josh nodded. It had been that already. He checked his watch. Nearly three. So he *would* have to explain getting home early. The only thing to do, he supposed, was tell the truth and hope.

When they turned down his street and he saw his house, Josh sighed. It hasn't changed since this morning, he thought. Of course not. He'd almost expected home to look different, he wasn't sure why. Maybe because he felt so different. But there it was, a perfectly ordinary two-story brick colonial house in the rain, surrounded by its mowed lawn, the leaves of its two crape myrtle trees just turning orange. "That's it."

"You expected?" Rafferty asked.

"Sure," Josh said, his voice carefully casual.

Rafferty stopped the truck. "Okay, kid, you're on your own."

Josh got out and stood for a moment with his hand on the truck door. "Thanks for the lunch. And the chance to meet Grock."

"You're welcome. Only you met Grock on your own. See you around!"

Josh slammed the door and Rafferty pulled away, waving a hand as the truck turned the corner.

Ducking his head against the rain, Josh ran around the side of the house to the back door, where Nimbus had begun to bark her greeting.

· 7 ·

JOSH DROPPED HIS JACKET and backpack by the door and began patting, scratching, and rubbing Nimbus into settling down. Apparently she had not barked long enough or loud enough to be heard upstairs. He gave her a dog biscuit and went to listen at the foot of the steps. Beethoven's *Eroica* Symphony boomed down the stairs at him. His mother had the volume up so high she probably hadn't even noticed Nimbus barking. And so high that if he went up to her studio now, she wouldn't hear him coming and would be startled out of her mind. He'd just have to outshout Beethoven and hope for the best. "Mom, I'm home!"

For a moment he thought he hadn't managed to make himself heard. There was no sound other than the music. But then it stopped abruptly and his mother appeared in the hallway above him in her paint-stained jeans and sweat shirt, her face a portrait of bewildered surprise. "You're early! Or is my watch screwed up again?"

Josh put on his best grin. "Nope. I'm early. You want to come down and have a cup of tea?"

"I'm not really at a good stopping place. . . ."

"Okay," Josh said. "I'll put the teakettle on anyway, and when you get to a stopping place, you can come down." He turned toward the kitchen.

"Wait. What are you doing home so early?"

Josh turned back, carefully maintaining his grin. "Well, see—I thought we could sort of talk about that over a nice, hot cup of tea."

His mother frowned. "Joshua, child of my heart, why do I get intimations of catastrophe from that smile?"

"It's your artist's soul. You're always good at picking up vibrations."

Her frown deepened. "I gather this was not an early dismissal day that I just forgot. And you don't *look* sick." She came down the steps and put her hand on his forehead. "Joshie, you're soaking wet!"

"Tea?" he asked sweetly.

She laughed and shook her head. "My son, the con artist. Okay. I assume the vibrations I'm picking up are not entirely joyful?"

"Cosmic," Josh said. "Cosmic is what they are."

She followed him into the kitchen. *The truth*, Josh thought, as he put the teakettle on. The truth, whatever that was. Or maybe just part of it for now. "We sure needed the rain," he said and got out the assortment of

56

herbal teas. "What'll you have, orange, apple, or al-mond?"

"Apple, please. Are we only allowed to talk about the weather?"

"Until the tea's ready." He climbed onto the kitchen stool and got an unopened box of gingersnaps out of the cupboard over the stove. "I hope it doesn't really storm, though. I'd hate to have all the leaves blown down now that they've finally changed color."

"The oak outside my window is going gold," his mother said, sitting at the kitchen table and leaning her elbows on the checked tablecloth. "But it isn't all that gorgeous today. It needs sun. Half the beauty of autumn is in the light."

"At least you don't have to worry about oak leaves blowing off in a storm. Did you know that regular oaks are direct descendents of live oaks? That's why they keep their leaves longer than any other deciduous trees. And that's why their leaves are so leathery— almost like magnolias. Oaks are as close to evergreens as they can get."

"My son, the botanist."

"A minute ago I was your son, the con artist. Which would you rather?"

"I never noticed I had much choice."

The teakettle began to whistle, and Josh took it off the heat. He pulled himself up to his greatest height and tried to sound like Dr. Ellsworthy. "I find labels limiting, especially when applied to children. Don't you?"

His mother didn't answer. She was looking at him steadily, and he had the sense that he was running out of delaying time. He busied himself with tea bags and mugs and took a moment to arrange the gingersnaps carefully on a plate. When there was nothing left to do, he set a mug in front of his mother, took his place at the table across from her, and sipped his tea, which burned his tongue and left him gasping. His mother stirred a spoonful of sugar into her mug and watched as he bit into a gingersnap. Finally, he swallowed. "I walked out of school today," he said, wishing his voice sounded more matter-of-fact.

"You walked out? In the middle of the day?"

"Yes."

"And how did you get home?"

"Well, partly I walked and partly I got a ride." Before his mother could get sidetracked onto the subject of who had given him a ride, he went on. "I can't go back there, Mom!"

His mother held her tea mug in front of her face, breathing in the apple and cinnamon aroma and gazing at him.

At least, he thought, her face hasn't closed up. She isn't angry—yet. "I really mean it. I can't go back on Monday. Or ever." He took another bite of gingersnap. He could hardly taste it. Nimbus pawed his knee, and he gave her the hand signal to lie down. She looked mutinous for a moment, then dropped to the floor and rested her chin on her paws, eyeing him forlornly.

Emily Forbes put down her mug. "You're telling me that you can't go back to the Everett School? Would you like to have a go at *why*?"

"It's not just the Everett School. I can't go back to school period. Not even if the police arrest me and take me to jail!"

She sighed. "If the police were going to arrest someone, Josh, it wouldn't be you."

"You mean they'd arrest you?"

"Yes. Or George. Maybe both of us. *When* did you walk out, by the way?"

"During math."

"Since I don't carry your schedule around in my head, how about giving me a time?"

"About eleven-thirty."

"And the school didn't call?" She started to rise from her chair, and Josh was afraid she would call the school that minute, but then she sank back and picked up a gingersnap. "It's my fault. They probably tried. I unplugged the phones. I had one of those aluminum siding calls again, and I got fed up. I *knew* I shouldn't do that, work or not. You could have been hurt—"

"But I wasn't."

59

"Still, I won't do that anymore."

Josh grinned. "You won't have to. From now on, I'll be home to take the aluminum siding calls."

"Not so fast, Josh. You're a ten-year-old boy."

"You remembered."

"Cute. Ten-year-old boys don't just come home and announce that they've quit school. It doesn't work that way. A fifth-grade dropout! I can just hear people now!"

"Don't, Mom!" Josh said. "Don't start thinking about anybody else. Don't think about what people would say or think. Just for now, please, please, just think about *me*."

"You. A ten-year-old child."

"Not *a* ten-year-old child, Mom. *This* one. Joshua Taylor, this particular ten-year-old child. Your son. If I were any other one, this conversation wouldn't be taking place."

His mother held her mug between her hands and stared out the rain-spattered windows into the heavy, gray sky. "Listen," she said finally, "I don't think I'm up to this conversation alone. And anyway, it's Friday. We have two whole days to talk about this—and think about it—before there's a day of school at all." He started to protest, but she held up one hand. "Two days. We're not going to make any final decisions, anyway, just the two of us. When George gets home, we can talk about it. You can tell us *why*, and we can talk

60

about it. Together." She sighed. "Meanwhile, I've got work to do . . . if I can do it after this. Oh, Joshie, however did you and I get stuck with each other?"

"Fate, I guess. Dreadful, blind fate!"

"Either that, or God thought we deserved each other!"

"Should I plug the phones back in?"

"Heavens, no! I don't want to take a chance that Dr. Ellsworthy will call *now*. We'll pretend we've gone to Acapulco for the weekend."

"Why pretend? Call George and we can leave right away!"

"There's a small matter of money, love." She stood up. "All afternoon I've been putting my heart and soul into drawing shoes, just to earn a little of that commodity—while drowning my brain in Beethoven. I have to get back to it. I'll be noble and refrain from mentioning the cost of the private school you just walked out of."

"Thanks."

"You're welcome. You and Nimbus go do your thing—no TV, please—and we'll talk later." She took her tea with her and turned back at the bottom of the steps. "And please put away the books you left in the family room last night, and your pens, and your paper, and anything else I may have missed tripping over. And hang up your jacket and backpack!"

Josh nodded. "Yes, ma'am." He stuffed a gingersnap

into his mouth and slipped one to Nimbus as soon as his mother started upstairs. "So far, so good," he whispered to the dog, who had swallowed her cookie whole. "Keep your paws crossed that George will be his usual cool, rational self tonight."

· 8 ·

Josh finished his bowl of ice cream, carefully scraping up the last of the chocolate sauce. Nimbus lay by the refrigerator, watching his every move, but she was going to be disappointed. He wasn't leaving any for her; he needed all the comfort he could get. He contemplated asking for another bowl but decided not to. They seldom had dessert anyway; to ask for seconds would be pushing his luck. They'd know he was stalling.

When George Forbes had come home, Josh had dutifully retired to his room to leave his parents alone. But he'd heard the drone of their voices as they worked together in the kitchen fixing dinner and knew they were talking about him, that his mother was telling George what he'd told her. Josh had tried reading for a while but found himself turning pages without the slightest idea of what he'd read. He might as well have had his eyes closed. Then he'd looked up the scientific name for crow: *Corvus brachyrhynchos.* He'd already

63

decided that telling Rafferty Grock's "real" name was a good enough excuse for going back there. He could row over in *Squeak* on Monday, if he didn't have to go back to school.

School. He'd tried, then, to plan what he would say to keep them from sending him back. It wasn't the time for joking. No clever cover-ups. But how could he put into words the desperation he was feeling? How could he make anyone, even his mother and George, understand? Maybe he shouldn't even try. Maybe he'd worn the camouflage so long he shouldn't take it off at all. Maybe he should just go back to school and try to cope. It must be what everyone else did! No matter what happened to him at school, Cole Simms was there every day, no matter how often he was teased and tormented about his size, his hair, his eyes, his glasses. But the thought of Cole had clinched it. He'd have to find a way to explain. He couldn't go back!

"So, shall we stay here or adjourn to the family room?" George asked.

Josh looked from his stepfather to his mother and back again. George was completely different from his real father, Emily always said. Phillip Taylor had been a would-be sculptor, a fine violinist, and utterly impulsive. Josh wondered sometimes how much besides his brown hair and green eyes he had inherited from his father. George was steady, logical, and reasonable, a professor of history who weighed all the facts carefully before making decisions. It was better that he had to face George with this than his father. He didn't need two parents who relied on their feelings. George was sitting impassively now, waiting, absently smoothing his graying moustache with one finger. Well, whatever would be decided tonight, these were his favorite two people in the world. If they couldn't understand, nobody could. If they couldn't understand, he was probably crazy. That was a possibility, he supposed. "Let's stay here," he said. "It's homier or something. And if you want more coffee, it's right here on the stove."

"You think this is going to be more than a one-cup discussion?"

Josh grinned. "Yes, sir. It'll take one cup just to get through why I walked out this morning."

So, while they drank their coffee, Josh did his best to explain. He told them the story of Matthew and the tiger swallowtail, of his disguise, and, leaving out the part about Cole Simms, he told of the crumbling of everything since that day in September when he'd had to leave the Tidewater summer, his dog, his boat, his books, and his river to go back to the airless classroom.

George listened, his face showing no emotion. Emily, however, fidgeted. She played with her coffee spoon, lifted her cup and set it down again without drinking, twisted her napkin. Josh had to avoid looking at her. He focused on Nimbus, as if he were telling everything to her and her alone, and managed to get

65

through the moment when Ms. Daniels's hand with its stubby bit of chalk had set him off, and he had found himself walking out.

"You say it's not just Ms. Daniels," George said. "A conflict with a teacher can cause a lot of problems."

Josh looked at the shredded remains of his mother's napkin and back at Nimbus. "No. It's me." He wished he'd given his ice cream to Nimbus after all. All of it. His stomach was clenched up again. He took a deep breath, willing his body to calm down.

"But, Josh, if you could just *try*—"

George's voice cut in. "No, Emily. He's telling us that he *has* tried. There's just so much you can ask of anyone."

"But you've seemed to get along with the other kids."

"That's the thing, Mom. I've *seemed* to. It's all been an act, and I just can't keep it up anymore."

"You just can't quit school," his mother said. "You've got a whole life to think of, not just this little piece of it. Nobody ever said school was perfect."

George laughed. "Except Thomas Ellsworthy."

"You know what I mean. We all have to do things we don't like. Do you think I *like* drawing shoes for a living?"

George looked at her for a moment. "Yes. At least you like it better than you'd like working in an office— or a bank—or teaching school."

"Well, that's not the same thing."

"Why? Because you're an adult?"

Emily pushed back her chair and went to the stove for the coffeepot. When she'd filled their cups, she stood for a moment looking out the window. Josh wondered if she could see the river in the darkness outside or only her own reflection. Then she turned back to face them, leaning against the counter. "Yes. Because I'm an adult. Because I went through all the things kids have to go through—all the school and all those years when I didn't have any choices."

George sighed. "You know what that reminds me of? Fraternity hazing. Every year freshmen go through all those clever horrors the upperclassmen think up for them. So that when they're upperclassmen they can say to the new freshmen that *they* got through it."

"You can't compare going to school with fraternity hazing!"

"Yes, I can. Think about it, Em. Hazing is designed to weed out the kids who won't fit the fraternity's image. Or the ones who don't care enough to get through it. Maybe school does the same thing. I'm not sure the main purpose is education, are you? Really?" When she didn't answer, he went on. "You wouldn't fit in an office. And I wouldn't fit at IBM. Why should Josh fit in school? Do we have any more right to be who we really are than he does, just because we're older?"

Josh wished he were back in his room. It would be easier to let them decide without him. His stomach was getting worse.

"And what would he do if he didn't go back? How would he learn? What if he wants to go to college, what then? I should think you, of all people, would stand up for education."

"That's exactly what I *do* stand up for. I'm just not convinced that a school is the best place for every kid to get an education. Would you like to read some of my students' history papers? Would you like to see what twelve years of school have done to educate them?"

"Would they have gotten a better education by dropping out?"

George held up one hand. "Wait, Emily. We're not talking about my students here. We're talking about Josh. This one person. Your son."

"Who is ten years old and who cannot be allowed to make a choice that could wreck his whole life."

George waved her to her chair. "Sit down, drink your coffee before it gets cold, and relax. I've got an idea."

Emily sat down, reluctantly. "All right, I'll listen. But I'm not guaranteeing anything."

"Suppose Josh had pneumonia."

"What?"

"Just stay with me. Suppose instead of walking out

of school today, he'd come home with pneumonia. Would you send him back to school Monday?"

"Of course not. What has that got to do with anything? He's perfectly healthy."

George looked at Josh and twitched his moustache. "What do you say, Josh? Are you healthy?"

Josh grinned and coughed, clutching his throat.

"There. You see? This sounds like a very sick boy. Dr. Forbes thinks it's pneumonia."

"Go on," Emily said.

"If Josh had pneumonia, he'd stay home until he got better, however long that took. So let us pretend for the moment that he's sick. He needs a leave of absence."

"But he'd get over pneumonia and go back. How long is this 'leave of absence' supposed to last?"

"Let's not decide that right now. Let's just say that whenever it ends, the Everett School is no longer an option. After five years there, I'd say he's given it a fair chance. Let's take the time to see what the alternatives are. It might be interesting. You never know till you start digging. Maybe we could hire a live-in Aristotle."

"Sure. They're a dime a dozen."

"We could always put an ad in the paper. What do they do when a kid *is* sick? Use tutors. They don't have to be Aristotle. Come on, Emily, don't tell me your artist's soul is afraid of being unconventional."

"If he had pneumonia, he'd be home and I'd have to

69

take care of him. I have an artist's soul, all right. What would happen to my work?"

"I won't interfere with that," Josh said. "Honest. You know I don't bother you when I come home from school and you're still working. Nimbus and I will stay out of your way, I promise. Won't we, girl?" Nimbus thumped her tail on the floor. "See? She promises, too!"

His mother shook her head. "I don't know. . . ."

"Pneumonia," George said. "Keep that in mind. This is a very sick boy."

"And what are we going to tell the school?"

"Leave that to me." George rubbed his chin. "I have several things I'd like to say to Thomas Ellsworthy that I've been biting back for five years. I'll call him first thing Monday morning."

"But—"

"No buts. A *temporary leave of absence*, while we figure out where to go from here. Meantime, Josh can do his own thing for a while."

His mother sighed a long, surrendering sigh. "All right. But I want you both to remember that this is a temporary condition, this pneumonia, and I'm going to do my very best to get it cured."

George twitched his moustache at Josh again. "Whad'ya say, Josh? Agreed?"

"Agreed!" Josh ruffled Nimbus's hair, and she thumped her tail again. "Nimbus agrees, too!"

· 9 ·

IT HAD BEEN A GOOD WEEKEND, Josh thought as he
rowed. Considering. They'd taken Nimbus walking in Seashore State Park on Sunday, looking like a
normal family. None of the people they'd passed on the
path could have guessed that the kid in their group was
a dropout, he was sure. His mother hadn't mentioned
school once, and if it sometimes seemed as if none of
them could think of anything to say, there wasn't any
real need to say anything most of the time. George had
pointed out a whole family, probably three generations, who looked so much alike they could have been
punched out with cookie cutters. Every one, down to a
girl who couldn't have been more than three, wore
horn-rimmed glasses. And Josh had found a fat skink,
shining in the sun like a piece of enameled jewelry.
Otherwise they'd just walked, each thinking separate
thoughts. They'd had pizza for dinner, then strolled the
beach while Nimbus frolicked in the water, snapping at

the waves. Josh had watched a sanderling with one badly mangled leg hop jerkily up and down the wave line and thought of Rafferty. Could Rafferty help this bird? Did it need help? It looked as if it could keep up with the others, as if it got as much to eat as they did.

Now it was Monday, the first real day of his "leave of absence," a sunny, hot fall day, and he was on his way to Rafferty's. He'd stayed in bed until nine, when Nimbus had finally gotten tired of waiting and licked him in the face until he had to get up to get away from her. George had already gone to teach his early class, and his mother had been in the kitchen when he went down, reading the morning paper. Josh had fixed himself a bowl of cereal and explained that he was going to pack a lunch and go out in *Squeak*.

"Watch the tide," she'd warned. "I don't want to worry about you getting stranded on a mud flat somewhere."

"I won't. Low tide's around noon. I'll go out now and come back when it's back up again. I found a place with a good channel, and I want to explore." He didn't tell her about Rafferty, for fear she'd forbid him to go. She'd probably worry either that Rafferty was crazy and dangerous or that he was a nice old man who didn't want Josh bothering him. Josh figured if Rafferty *didn't* want him around, he'd let him know it, but his mother might not believe that.

72

"All right," she'd said. "Don't forget to wear your—"

"Life vest. Yes, Mother. And I'll hang my clothes on the hickory limb, and I won't go near the water."

"Cute, Joshie, cute. I mean it. Be careful."

"Yes, ma'am. I always am. See you this afternoon."

"Are you taking Nimbus?"

"Not this time. I'll walk her when I get back." He didn't know what Nimbus would think of Grock or the other birds, and he didn't think today was the best time to find out. He wasn't all that sure Rafferty would want to see him, let alone his dog.

So he'd left Nimbus staring after him as he rowed away, her front feet on the bulkhead, wagging her tail and whining. By the time she had dwindled to a white spot against the background of his house, he'd gotten over feeling guilty about her.

His mother was right about water, Josh thought. She always said she needed to live on water because it soothed her soul and kept her sane. No matter how uptight she got, all she needed to do was sit out on the patio for a while, and things would slip into perspective. Dawn was her favorite time, when the sun wasn't high enough yet to clear the trees across the river but tinted the sky and the mist a pale pink. But any time would do, because the water was always changing, with the light or the wind or the seasons. She said that was why people were willing to pay more for houses on

73

water, even the little water of the creeks and inlets.

Josh looked at the yards he was passing. Each had its deck or patio or dock set with lounge chairs or picnic tables, surrounded by various kinds of outdoor lights. Some were screened and roofed, others were open to the sun and the mosquitos. The grass was mowed, the gardens planted with mums and marigolds. Leaves, when they fell, would be raked up quickly. Everything was carefully arranged to take advantage of the river, as if it had been put there solely for the house owners' pleasure.

But this water was not just for them! Josh thought. It was a whole world, a whole universe to more kinds of living things than most of them could even imagine. He stopped rowing for a moment, watching a jellyfish pulse to the surface, its white tentacles trailing gracefully behind it. "Stinging nettles" they were called by the people who wished to banish them from the bay and rivers. An ugly name for so elegant a creature. Another, smaller one came close to the boat. He rowed, trying to catch it in one of the whirlpools the oar made, but it merely turned itself upside down and disappeared into the dark water. Pretty as they were, of course, they did keep him from swimming here, no matter how hot the summers got. He hated jellyfish stings as much as anybody.

It was getting hot now, Josh thought. He'd been rowing for nearly an hour, and this was the third creek he'd tried without finding Rafferty's. He was sweating under his life vest and wished he could just take it off. He could swim, had learned to swim before he could walk. But he'd made an unbreakable promise to wear the life vest—the only way he could persuade his mother to let him explore in *Squeak* on his own. He supposed it was finally worth it.

He sighed. This creek, too, dwindled to a muddy trickle ahead. He turned the boat, letting it drift as he dug the thermos of apple juice out of his lunch bag and took a drink. He checked his watch and then laughed. The time didn't matter! There was no bus waiting for him. No bell would ring. He was free! His schedule was no more demanding than the tides. He had what he'd always wanted more than anything in the world—*time*.

As *Squeak* nosed out into the river again, he saw a cormorant, its long neck stretching up from the surface of the water like a periscope. Suddenly, with the tiniest of splashes, it ducked its head and disappeared. Josh began to count, sweeping his eyes back and forth over the water where it had vanished. As he was about to say "forty-three," the bird appeared again, yards closer. He rowed toward it, and it raised its wet body with an effort, flapping its wings and running awkwardly across the water until it finally lifted off, skimmed the surface, and landed with a shake of its body on a piling at the end of a ramshackle dock.

There was another creek ahead, larger than the last.

This one had to be it, he decided. Anyway, if it turned out not to be, he could still explore it. As he rowed he watched the water behind the boat, slicked down by his passage—a miniature wake. Three sea gulls flew over his head, one of them, a small fish in its beak, screaming like a woman being mugged. The others screamed back and dove at the fish. There was a brief scuffle of wings in the air and the three flew off, still screaming. Josh hadn't seen which bird finally got the prize. "Hoodlums!" he shouted after them. As if in answer, a loud cawing erupted behind him.

So he'd found the place at last! Josh rowed more quickly, throwing splashes of water into the boat near his feet. He looked over his shoulder and spotted Rafferty's dock, just as a black shape hurtled from the shadows under the trees, heading directly for him. He ducked, and the crow landed on the nets and lunch bag on the stern seat. The bird had recognized him! It had actually come out to greet him! "Hi," he said.

"Hello, hello," Grock answered. Josh laughed and rowed more gently now to avoid splashing the bird as it investigated his gear, eyeing everything and making experimental pecks. Josh reached for the lunch bag, tugging it slightly.

"If you'll just get off, I've got something for you." Grock hopped to the edge of the boat and watched while Josh rummaged in the bag and pulled out a cookie. "Here," he said, breaking a piece off. "It's a gingersnap. You want it?" He held it out.

"Chow time!" the crow said. It blinked and hopped closer, then took the cookie from his hand. Josh fed it three more pieces and popped the last bit into his own mouth.

"Now you've done it!" Josh turned to see Rafferty standing on his dock, his hands on his hips. "He won't leave you alone until he's tasted everything you have. Feeding a crow cookies! You want to wreck his diet?"

"*Corvus brachyrhynchos* is an omnivore," Josh said, using his best Ellsworthy voice, "eating everything from grain to berries to the young of other birds to carrion. So a gingersnap couldn't hurt," he added in his own voice.

"Hasn't anybody ever warned you about being a smart-ass kid?"

"Lots of people," Josh said, rowing toward the dock.

"I suppose that cute-little-boy grin is supposed to make up for it, huh?"

Did the man have a window into his mind? "Doesn't it?"

"Not for me. I once saw a kid with a grin just like that set fire to a kitten. I kicked that kid's blue-jeaned rear halfway to the next county—grin or no grin."

Josh stared at Rafferty, open-mouthed, while *Squeak* bumped solidly into the dock, sending Grock into the air with an irate squawk. The crow flew off to his dogwood tree, muttering to himself. "Easy! Easy!" Rafferty said, putting the toe of his boot on *Squeak*'s prow. "This dock isn't much, but it should last me a while yet." He held out his hand. "Toss me your line."

"Is that true? About the kitten?"

"Of course it's true. I don't invent stories to make a point." Rafferty bent to secure the line to a corroded cleat on the dock. "By the time you've lived as long as I have, you'll know there's not a story a man can think up that hasn't been told—good or bad—in real life." Rafferty straightened, groaning, and put a hand on the small of his back.

"Are you okay?"

"Sure. A little stiff is all. I spent half the night on the water last night—and the damp got into the old joints."

"Half the night?"

"I was picking up a new patient. Listen, I don't know why you happened over here this morning, but your timing's terrific. I need an extra pair of hands right now, and it'll save a lot of time if I don't have to go out looking for them."

Josh grinned. "I'll be glad to help."

"Okay, then. Let's have your chow and I'll put it in the fridge. Grock can get into anything but a time-locked safe."

While Rafferty took his lunch bag into the house, Josh stood in the yard, looking around. He'd almost convinced himself that he'd dreamed this place. But here it was, the same as before. The heron with the bandaged wing gazed imperiously at him from its pen. The peg-legged sea gull stood next to the water pail, apparently sulking. But the smaller pen was empty.

"Where are the turtles?" Josh asked when Rafferty came back outside.

"Gone. I took them out to the woods over the weekend. I only hang onto them long enough to make sure they're okay. I picked those two up on the Interstate. Last of the season, I hope." He glanced up at the sky. "If it stays as warm as this, I'll probably find some more. Turtles never seem to learn the difference between sunbathing on a rock and sunbathing on a road."

"Box turtles make great pets," Josh said.

Rafferty shook his head. "I don't believe in wild pets. Dogs, sure. Cats. Even hamsters, if they don't bore you to death. Not wild things." Josh glanced at Grock. "He's no pet. He's just a friend who happens to like my company. He's free to leave any time. A crow can make it fine with only one good foot. Most birds can."

"Then why . . . ?"

"I told you, he's weird. You know Saint Francis?"

"Not personally."

"Smart-ass! Saint Francis took up with animals. Well, Grock's sort of a backwards Saint Francis. He took up with me. He talks to crows sometimes, when they come around and try to persuade him to remember who he is and come back. He even flies with them sometimes. But he doesn't seem to want to join them permanently. Not so far, anyway."

"Will he migrate?"

"I don't know. Maybe someday. It's a free country."

"He said 'chow time' when I fed him. I thought crows didn't understand what they say."

"That's what I've always said when I feed him. It's association. The next best thing to understanding." Rafferty looked around the yard. "You haven't been introduced to the others. The great blue's name is Gainsborough."

"Gainsborough?"

"You ever hear of a painting called *The Blue Boy*? It's by an artist named Gainsborough."

"Oh."

"You want to guess the gull's name?"

Josh thought a moment. He didn't know what Rafferty might call him, but he knew what *he* would. "Long John Silver?"

"I knew there was something I liked about you. Never was a meaner tempered pirate."

"Does he need that peg leg?"

"Not anymore. I just fixed that up for him when his leg had to be amputated, until the stump healed and he got used to balancing. But he's a malingerer. Every time I take it off, he falls over. I think he's hooked on being fed for free. One of these days I'll take it off and just let him lie on the ground until he's ready to give up the game." He waved his hand toward the cages. "The kingfisher's Richard the Second and the mallard's Lucky—"

"As in Ducky-Lucky?"

"Never mind. That gull's name is Attila."

Josh looked into the cage. The gull looked back with a gaze that seemed full of fury. "I can see why."

"All right, you've met the outpatients. Now, you really want to work? Seriously?" Josh nodded. "Okay. This way to Intensive Care."

· 10 ·

I T HAD BEEN A GARAGE, Josh saw, as he looked around the bright, gleaming white room. But there was no room for a car in it now. The big door had been replaced by a wall with three small windows near the ceiling. Beneath the windows were four stacks of fiber glass cages made for transporting animals. They were different sizes, with the largest on the bottom and the smallest on the top. Each had a wire door with a small clipboard hanging on it. "Charts," Josh said, "just like in a hospital."

"It is a hospital," Rafferty said.

Josh looked into one of the lower cages. It contained a gigantic black-backed gull with a broken wing. The clipboard said the bird's name was Stanley, that its wing had been set on September 20th and antibiotics given until the first week in October. "Did you set its wing?"

"Pickett does the veterinary work. Dr. Pickett—a

buddy of mine. We have a sort of informal partnership. He does the doctoring and I do everything else!"

"Doesn't it get expensive?" Josh's mother had complained the last time they'd taken Nimbus to the vet because the visit and one shot had cost twenty-four dollars.

"Pickett works free, but everything else costs an arm and a leg."

Some of the cages were empty, Josh saw. "Do you ever get full in here?"

"Full and more, sometimes. I keep the old wood cages I used to use in case there's an overflow. Summer's the worst time. More people are out then. Winter has its own problems, though."

Along one other wall were white metal cupboards and a counter with a stainless steel top. In the center of the room was a large table, also topped with stainless steel. Next to the table stood a wooden crate covered with an old bedspread. "The new kid on the block," Rafferty said, putting his hand on it. "An egret." He picked up a bucket next to the crate. "Only a crazy person would try to force-feed an egret by himself."

"Force-feed?"

"This fella could go for a while without eating, but I have to get an antibiotic into him, and this is the best way." Rafferty took a bottle off the counter and shook a pill into his hand. Then he grabbed a baitfish out of the bucket and pushed the pill into the fish's mouth. He tossed Josh a pair of safety goggles. "Put these on. An egret's beak could take your eye out before you even think about turning your head. Now, I'll stuff this fish down its gullet, and you take it the rest of the way, while I hold the beak."

"Huh?"

"You squeeze the fish down, like pushing an orange down into the toe of a sock. Just squeeze gently from above and keep working it down until it gets into the chest and you can't feel it anymore."

"Can't it swallow on its own?"

"It *can*. But a force-fed egret'll just upchuck again if you don't get the food down far enough. Does it anyway, sometimes. Birds swallow up as easy as down. But this one needs the medicine, so we have to try."

Josh put the goggles on and wiped his hands on his jeans. He'd never been close to an egret before, except at the zoo, and that was very different.

Rafferty pulled back the bedspread. "The dark keeps it calmer," he explained and opened the top of the crate. Immediately a sharp yellow beak struck upward. Rafferty, apparently expecting it, grabbed the beak quickly and held it for a few seconds. Then he gently pried it open and put the fish into the gaping mouth. The bird eyed them coldly.

"I don't think he likes this," Josh said. Up close the bird looked a great deal more dangerous than it did stalking gracefully along the tideflats. Out there egrets looked almost fragile.

"You wouldn't like somebody stuffing food down your throat either. Go ahead now. I've got him."

Gingerly, Josh reached out and grasped the bird's neck. The feathers were soft and smooth—silky—but the slender throat felt surprisingly strong. The fish was a lump he could feel easily. He began to push it down. It wasn't quite like squeezing an orange into a sock, more like squeezing something through a garden hose. Finally, the fish slipped far enough that he could no longer feel it. He kept his hand on the white breast for a moment, then looked up. Rafferty nodded. "That should do it. I'll hold its beak for a while to make sure we don't get the fish back."

Josh took his hand away and looked at the bird. Its wings seemed all right. "What happened to it?"

"Check out the legs."

In the dim depths of the crate, Josh could see deep gashes below the knee joints on both black legs. "What did that?"

"Monofilament fishing line. Happens all the time. Fisherman gets a backlash or a snag and just cuts the line off his reel. The damn stuff doesn't disintegrate. Wading birds get tangled in it and can't get loose. The stuff cuts like a knife. Sometimes they fly off, dragging the line. Then it gets snagged on something. Mostly they die."

"How'd you find this one?"

"Got a call. He was spotted hanging in a tree, upside down."

"You got the call during the night?"

"Late yesterday afternoon. I waited till it got dark. You can shine a light in their eyes when it's dark and they'll hold still while you cut them loose. Otherwise they get into a frenzy trying to get away. They can cripple themselves permanently and tear hell out of you, too. That's why it's better to have two people. But none of the guys I usually get to help could come along last night." Rafferty closed the crate, letting go of the bird's beak at the last minute. The egret didn't try to strike again. Rafferty put the bedspread back over the crate. "I'll keep it in the dark for a while longer. Then we can transfer it to one of the big cages."

"You going to name this one?" Josh asked.

"I name them all. It's easier to keep track of them that way. *You* want to think up a name?"

"Is it a male or female?"

"Good question. Another egret could tell, but I can't. There's a woman who does wildlife rehabilitation in North Carolina who swears by the ring trick."

"What's that?"

"You put a gold ring on a thread and hold it like a pendulum over the animal's head. After a little, it starts to move. If it moves in a circle, the animal's a female, and if it moves back and forth, it's a male. She says she learned the trick from an old mountain woman."

"Does it work?"

"Like I say, she swears by it. I think it's like finding water with a dousing rod, highly suspect. Anyway, it doesn't really matter, does it? Except to another egret."

"I guess not. How about Snow White?"

"Very original."

"Have you used it before?"

Rafferty laughed. "Never mind, kid. Pickett tells me I'm a sarcastic old so-and-so. Don't let it bother you."

Josh shrugged. "I won't. Is Snow White going to be okay, do you think?"

"Probably. I don't keep them if they don't have any chance."

"How do you know?"

"You know. Most of the time."

"And what if they don't have a chance? What do you do then?"

Rafferty took the bait bucket to an old soft-drink cooler next to the door and put it in. Then he turned back. "Anything that starts out alive has to die sometime. It's a good idea to remember that. Not a bad job you did, for a beginner."

"Thanks. It was fun."

"Can't say that's the word I'd use. Most of this business is work. Do you have anything against work?"

"That depends on what kind," Josh said as casually as possible.

"I've got a couple of other jobs you could do for me

around here—like cleaning out cages. If you don't have any other pressing concerns."

"Okay!" Josh said. "Okay!"

For the next hour, under Rafferty's exacting eye, Josh cleaned cages, learned the names of the birds, and read their charts. He listened eagerly to the stories of their injuries, their illnesses, their capture. When Rafferty looked at his watch and announced that it was well past lunchtime, Josh was surprised. He couldn't remember a morning that had passed so quickly.

They ate in the kitchen, Grock sitting outside in the dogwood, pointedly watching them through the screen door and announcing from time to time that it was chow time. When Josh finished, except for a cookie he'd saved for Grock, he glanced at Rafferty, who was eating an apple and looking at him. "You haven't asked why I'm not in school."

"Figured you'd tell me if you wanted me to know."

Josh nodded. He doubted there was another adult in the world who would say such a thing. "I'm taking what George, my stepfather, calls a 'leave of absence.'"

"I took a leave of absence once, from the Navy. They didn't call it that, though."

"Well"—Josh grinned—"I don't think school calls it that, either."

"Your idea or theirs?"

"Mine. I just had to get out of there. Was your leave from the Navy your idea?"

"I'd say so. What the Navy called it was 'absent *without* leave.' "

"Isn't that serious?"

Rafferty laughed. Outside, Grock laughed too, and the sounds were so much alike that Josh couldn't help joining them. "Let's just say that I parted from the Navy on less than friendly terms. It wasn't pleasant, but it was a lot better than staying in the Navy. Funny thing was, I'd joined the Navy because high school didn't agree with me."

"Didn't you finish high school?"

"Eventually. High school, college, graduate school, the whole bit. I just didn't do it the ordinary way or at the ordinary time is all." Rafferty squinted at Josh. "Did the school's uniform get to you?"

"We didn't have uniforms. . . ."

"Not clothes. I mean the mental uniform. Is that what got you?"

Josh shrugged. He hadn't thought of it that way. "I guess. I didn't fit very well. I'm not much like the other guys. And I don't think I want to be."

"What grade? Seventh?"

Josh flushed. "No. Just fifth."

Rafferty dropped his apple core into his napkin. "Fifth? How old are you?"

"Ten."

"Good God. I thought you were older than that. I figured you were just short."

Josh sat up very straight. "What difference does it make?"

"Relax, kid. It doesn't make any difference, really. Just shows my own mental uniform."

"Didn't I do things right today?"

"Sure you did. I told you that. But I'm not used to thinking a ten-year-old's up to taking much responsibility."

"People think ten-year-olds are all the same—and thirteen-year-olds—and—"

"Hey, I said relax. Kids aren't any more alike than anybody else, obviously. Adults tend to forget it sometimes. So how long is this 'leave of absence' going to last?"

Before Josh could answer, a voice came from the backyard. "Rafferty! Rafferty! Get out here!" Rafferty went to the door.

"Don't yell so loud, Tucker! You'll rupture your gut and scare hell out of the birds."

"I don't give a damn about those birds, Rafferty! That thieving crow of yours has been at it again."

Rafferty motioned to Josh to stay where he was. "My neighbor," he whispered. He opened the door and stepped out. Grock landed on his shoulder.

"Bad dog! Bad dog!" Grock screamed. "Get out!"

"Well, Tucker," Rafferty said. "What now?"

· 11 ·

As he rowed home, Josh looked at the familiar banks along the river as if he'd never seen them before. Everything looked different. The voices of the gulls overhead seemed less quarrelsome than usual, and the sun lit everything with an orangey glow that seemed to add to the transformation. Rafferty had offered him a job. There wouldn't be any money in it, of course; Rafferty had barely enough extra for food and medicine for the birds. But that didn't matter. There wasn't any money in school either. George and his mother just *had* to let him work with Rafferty. It would solve the problem of what to do with him during the day after all. Today had been a day like no day he'd ever known.

After lunch, they'd had to deal with Tucker first. Tucker, the man who owned the brick house next door, hated Rafferty's birds, apparently hated Rafferty. But most of all, he hated Grock. The crow seemed to return the feeling and lost no chance to make it clear.

This time he had gotten into the shed in Tucker's backyard and had taken everything out of his fishing tackle box, scattering it around the floor, and apparently stealing his favorite lure. "Crows can't resist shiny things," Rafferty had told the man. "I've warned you to keep that shed locked up." Finally Rafferty had given Tucker enough money to replace the lure, and the man had gone away, still grumbling.

"The man's a maniac." Rafferty said after he'd left. "If I can't get Grock to leave him alone, he's going to do something. Poison him, maybe."

"He wouldn't!" Josh protested.

"Don't kid yourself. The man thinks of everything as good—for him. Or bad—for him. Anything that's bad for him deserves to be gotten rid of, like the dandelions in his precious lawn."

"But he wouldn't really poison Grock, would he?"

Rafferty shrugged. "Maybe not. That would be too direct. Tucker's devious; if he takes it into his head to go after me, I don't think he'd settle for killing Grock."

"Can't you do anything?"

"Not until *he* does something. Sometimes I think he leaves that shed open on purpose so he can come over and raise hell. Anyway, I can't keep Grock away from him. Crows know who they like and who they don't, and you don't want to be on their enemy list. You could do a lot worse, though, than to pick your friends according to a crow's preferences."

Rafferty had had errands to run in the afternoon,

and Josh went along, to a hardware store, to Dr. Pickett's office to get some pills, and to fishing piers for the baitfish Rafferty used to feed the birds. Everywhere they went Rafferty took time to talk to people, starting every conversation with an insult. Josh was embarrassed at first, but nobody seemed offended. They all just laughed, and some of them insulted him back. Then he'd ask about their families and friends. Josh had the feeling that Rafferty knew everyone in the world and everyone knew him.

At the second fishing pier the man who brought out a battered ice chest full of fish nodded over his shoulder into the depths of the bait house. "Got one for you today, Raff."

"Have those barbarians of yours done it again?"

The man nodded. "I didn't call, 'cause I knew you were coming in today."

In a box in the corner of the bait house was a cormorant, a lure with three sets of hooks firmly embedded in its beak and neck. A few inches of fishing line dangled from the lure. Rafferty talked softly to the bird, who stayed quiet in the box. "That's a bad one, fella. Guess we'd better see what we can do." He turned to the man. "Has he been calm like this the whole time?"

"He went after the guy who pulled him in, but otherwise he's been pretty much like that. Just sits there, almost as if he's been waiting for you."

"Maybe he has."

When they got back to Rafferty's, they unloaded the cormorant first, taking his box to the table in the garage. Rafferty gave Josh the safety goggles again. "Cormorants have a hook of their own on those beaks. Plenty dangerous." But the precautions turned out to be unnecessary. The bird remained perfectly calm, letting itself be lifted out of the box and set on the table, holding completely still while Rafferty cut the barbs off the fishhooks in its beak. The tip of the hook in its neck was under the skin. "You hold his beak for me now," Rafferty said. "This could stir him up a little. And don't be afraid to be firm. I don't want him getting loose." As Josh held the bird's beak, Rafferty gently worked the hook's barb forward and pushed it through the skin. Josh winced as the point came through, bringing with it a drop of blood. "Always work a hook forward, even if you have to make a new wound. You try working it backward and that barb'll tear everything up." He clipped the barb off with his wire cutters, then worked the rest of the hook backwards and out, and dropped the lure into the trash can. "At least the guys at the piers know now not to just cut the birds loose with hooks in them. When a fisherman does that, the bird dies, sure as sure." He dusted antibiotic powder on the wounds, then placed the unprotesting bird in the end cage of the bottom row. "Could still lose this one," he said as he closed the wire door.

"He looks okay to me," Josh said.

"Hooks can cause infection." Rafferty wiped off the

counter, put the wire cutters and the antibiotic powder away, and then narrowed his eyes at Josh. "Listen, kid. Trying to save birds is no sure thing. It's more like roulette. The odds are against you. If you can't take that, you'd better not get into it."

"But you said you can tell which ones are going to make it. . . ."

"What I meant was that I can usually tell when an injury is likely to cripple a bird for life. I'm doing a very small job here. I can't keep up with the injuries during the busy times; I just don't have room to house birds that'll never be able to make it on their own again. This place is no zoo. If infection doesn't get this fella, he'll make it. He won't be crippled. Either he'll die or he'll go back to his old life. Meantime, I've done what I can." Josh hadn't thought about one of the birds dying. "So. Can you take the possibility we might lose him?"

"I guess I'll have to, won't I?"

"I guess you will."

And then it had been time to start home. The tide was already past high and falling again, and it was getting chilly. He was grateful for his life vest now. He could hear Nimbus barking; he was nearly home. He glanced over his shoulder as he rowed and saw his mother standing next to Nimbus, the binoculars she kept on the kitchen windowsill around her neck.

"Joshua Phillip Taylor," she called. "Where have you been? Do you know it's nearly 6:00?"

"I told you I'd be back with the tide!"

"The tide beat you."

He rowed up against the bulkhead and Nimbus leapt into the boat, nearly dumping him out, and licked his face. He pushed her off and put on his most innocent grin. "Sorry I worried you, Mom. It won't happen again."

"A likely story." His mother looped *Squeak*'s line around a piling when he tossed it to her. "Maybe you'd better install a ship-to-shore radio in *Squeak*."

"I've got a better idea," Josh said and tossed the oars onto the grass. "I'll give you a number where you can call me. I've got a new friend."

"You've found another dropout?"

"I didn't say he was a kid." Josh shoved Nimbus ahead of him and climbed over the bulkhead. "He's retired, I think. Anyway, he offered me a job."

"A job? I thought dropouts were supposed to loiter on street corners, not take jobs. Doing what?"

"Is George home?"

"Yes. Doing what, Josh?"

"Why don't I tell you both at once? You know, another family conference."

His mother sighed and took Josh's lunch bag while he carried the oars. "You think you need George, do you? Maybe Nimbus and I had better form a girls' team."

"No," Josh said, hoping he was right. "Everybody's going to agree this time."

So, while George and his mother fixed dinner, Josh told them about Rafferty and Grock and Gainsborough and Long John Silver. He told them about force-feeding the egret and holding the cormorant's beak and about Dr. Pickett and the man at the fishing pier. He didn't mention Tucker.

"And I suppose this Mr. Rafferty—"

"Just Rafferty," Josh corrected. "He insists."

"I suppose this 'Rafferty' also walks on water."

"I haven't seen him try. . . ."

"But you wouldn't put it past him."

"So? Can I work with him? He could really use an assistant. Or an apprentice."

"What do you think, Em?" George asked. "Sounds like a constructive use of time."

"George, we don't even know the man."

"True."

"You'll love him!" Josh said. "I know you will. Everybody does. We could invite him over so you can both meet him."

"Well . . ." Emily said.

George took the phone book from its drawer and dropped it on the table in front of Josh. "Call him and ask if he can drop over tonight. He sounds like someone worth meeting anyway."

"No promises!" Emily said.

"Right." Josh flipped the pages toward *R*, wanting to laugh. If they met Rafferty, they'd have to agree!

"Why don't you bring them over here instead," Rafferty suggested when Josh had delivered his invitation. "That way I can give them the grand tour."

"Great!" Josh said. "And they can meet Grock."

"That'll be up to Grock. Bring 'em over this evening, if it's all right. About eight."

"Okay. Eight o'clock. We'll be there!"

All the way to Rafferty's that evening, Josh worried. What would they think of his house? Of the long grass and the rattletrap truck in the driveway? What was the inside like? Josh had only been in the kitchen. At least that was clean. The garage, of course, had to impress them. That was spotless. And what would they really think of Rafferty? Would he start off by insulting them the way he did the man at the lumberyard and the receptionist at Dr. Pickett's office? Would they understand that he was only joking, that it was only his way of breaking the ice?

When Rafferty came to the door, Josh sighed with relief. He had practically dressed up. At least he'd put a string tie on his plaid shirt and changed his work pants for corduroy trousers. And he'd combed his hair back so that it looked only long and not straggly and unkempt the way it looked sticking out from under his old baseball cap. The hand he held out was clean, and the smile he turned on Emily when they shook hands was warm and welcoming.

"I'm pleased to meet you," she said.

"You'd better wait and see how pleased you are," Rafferty said. But before she could react, he went on. "I thought Josh was probably exaggerating when he told me what a beautiful mother he had. Not so. You," he said to George, "have been billed not as beautiful, but wise."

"I think that means that I often agree with Josh," George said as the men shook hands.

Rafferty ushered them into the living room, and Josh couldn't help smiling at what he saw. If he'd built the room like a stage set between the phone call and this moment, it couldn't have been better. The two walls without windows were covered from floor to ceiling with bookcases, into which books had been packed so tightly it would have been hard to squeeze a sheet of paper in. On top of the books were others, stacked sideways. The furniture was old and worn: a sagging couch, two easy chairs, and a trunk serving as a coffee table. The floor was bare wood, stained and dull. But in the center of the room was a rug the likes of which Josh had never seen. It was woven of some heavy, knobbly yarn, the color of bone. An asymmetrical pattern was woven into it in browns and tans and a deep rust. Emily had stopped in the archway, looking at the rug.

"That's handmade, isn't it," she said. It wasn't really a question. "Did you do it?"

Rafferty waved one dismissive hand. "Not I. I

couldn't do something like that if they made it in a kit. No, my wife made it."

Wife? Josh didn't know Rafferty had a wife. He realized that he knew almost nothing about the man.

"She did those, too," Rafferty added, following Emily's eyes to the intricately knotted cords covering the windows. "She had to work hard to make the place liveable with me around. She was some woman." He stared at the curtains for a moment. "She died three years ago."

"I'm sorry," Emily said.

"So am I." He motioned them to seats. "What can I get you? Coffee? Beer? Wine? Something hard?"

George and Emily both asked for wine, and Rafferty disappeared into the kitchen. "He's certainly a reader," George said.

"These aren't best sellers, either," Emily said, scanning the spines of the books nearest her. "Thoreau, Krutch, Mattheissen, Eisley, Lorenz, Leopold. . . ."

"Poetry here," George said. "There's Eliot and Stevens and Pound, for heaven's sake." Josh didn't know who those poets were, but he could see that his parents were impressed. To think he'd asked Rafferty if he'd finished high school!

"Here we are," Rafferty said, returning with a tray of glasses and a plate of cheese and crackers. "Sorry about the glasses. I haven't a whole set of anything."

"Variety's nice," Emily said, taking a glass of wine. "Thank you."

"Cider for you," Rafferty said. He winked at Josh as he handed him a glass.

"Thanks."

"Quite a library you have here," George said.

"Not particularly catholic, I'm afraid. I know what I like, I like what I like, and to hell with the rest."

"You like poetry."

"Ah, no. That was my wife again. I can't make head nor tail of half of them. Especially her favorites. That caused an argument or two. What I like are the naturalists—the world's best philosophers, some of them."

The adults talked for a while, as Josh sat, sipping his cider and not listening. He hoped Rafferty would avoid mentioning the Navy and keep his language under control. His mother had to be won over. He had a feeling that if Rafferty's wife were still alive, he'd be home free already.

"How about the inspection tour?" Rafferty said at last. "You can't make up your mind about letting Josh help me without seeing what I do."

He began with the garage, introducing them to the patients and showing them the wildlife rehabilitation permit that allowed him to handle migratory birds. He told them about his informal partnership with Dr. Pickett. Then he took them to the backyard, turning on the floodlights and waking Grock, who voiced his objections in no uncertain terms and refused to emerge from his box in the dogwood. Rafferty explained that the birds in the outdoor pens were in the last stages of convalescence and were free to fly away as soon as they were able. "It takes some transition time to get them back on their own. Luckily, my location lets them go directly from here back to wherever they belong."

When they returned to the living room, Rafferty refilled the glasses. "So what's the verdict? Do I get an apprentice?"

"This is quite an operation you have here," George observed.

"It's not enough. But I do what I can."

"How long have you been doing it?" Emily asked.

"Not long. Only three years full time. Zena and I used to take care of an occasional mallard with a broken wing. After she was gone, it just seemed like the thing to do. Pickett pushed a little, I'd have to admit. Well? Can Josh help?"

Josh held his breath and sent out psychic orders to his mother: *say yes, say yes, say yes.*

"Yes," Emily said. It had worked! "But only till he goes back to school."

"Suits me. How about it, Josh?"

"Great!" It was hard to keep himself on the couch. What he really wanted to do was jump around the room and hug people.

As they were leaving, Emily asked about the front door. "It's from a beach house we had once," Rafferty said. "Hurricane took the house. The only thing left when we got back was this door—leaning against a brand new sand dune. Zena couldn't stand to lose that door. We never had another beach house, but the door went with us ever after. Of course, it didn't always fit the house!"

As they drove home, Josh said nothing, listening vaguely to his parents talk about Rafferty's work. He could hardly believe he had met the man only days before. He felt as if he'd known him always. There were plenty of things he didn't know about him, but it didn't matter. Like Grock, Josh knew enough. Like Grock, Josh wanted to stay.

· 12 ·

FOR THE REST OF THE WEEK Josh worked with Rafferty, cleaning cages, feeding birds, helping to repair the outdoor shelters in preparation for winter, and answering the phone when Rafferty had to be away. Once he rowed over in *Squeak*, but the other days George dropped him at Rafferty's before he went to the university. On those days Rafferty took him home in the late afternoon. When he wasn't working, Josh talked to Grock, trying to teach the crow to say his name, or just watched the birds, sometimes talking to them, too, encouraging them to get well. On Wednesday they removed the bandage from Gainsborough's wing and the heron began moving around the pen, occasionally stretching its wings out and folding them back again, as if trying them. "Looks perfect," Rafferty said. "You can never be *sure* about how a wing will heal."

"Will he fly away now?"

"When he's ready."

That afternoon Rafferty tried removing Long John Silver's wooden leg again, and this time the bird didn't fall on its side. Instead, it balanced itself with its wings, then stood on its one leg and glared at them malevolently. When Josh left, the gull was hopping grumpily around the pen, screaming at the heron from time to time and complaining, Rafferty said, that no one ever gave him enough to eat. The next day—a brilliant, brisk fall day—Long John seemed grumpier than ever and as restless as the heron. Finally, while Rafferty and Josh were transferring Stanley the gull to an outdoor cage, Long John flew out of the pen, circled a few times over the water and back, landed once on the roof of the house, and then flew away, screaming a last, irritated farewell. "Can't say I'm sorry to see that one go," Rafferty said. Looking at Gainsborough standing in the pen alone, Josh missed Long John already.

On Friday, Josh woke to rain and a serious chill in the air. "Wear your raincoat," his mother warned, as he and George were leaving. "And a sweater. You won't go out on the water today, will you?"

"Not unless there's an emergency."

"Well, don't let there be one." Emily poured herself a cup of coffee and sat down at the table as Josh zipped his raincoat. "And get home in time to take Nimbus for a walk, okay? With all this attention to birds, you've been neglecting her."

Josh nodded and smiled angelically. "Anything else, Mother dear?"

She grinned and threw the still folded newspaper at him. "Go on and get out of here. Just be sure to keep Nimbus in mind."

When he got to Rafferty's, Josh went first to see Grock and take him a cookie. As Rafferty had said, Grock didn't like the rain. He was hunched in his box, looking miserable. "You could go inside if you weren't such a stinker," Josh told him. The one time he'd been inside the garage since his foot healed, Rafferty had said, he'd gotten into the medicine cabinet and thrown everything out onto the counter. Replacing the supplies had cost a fortune and Grock had lost a chance for a comfortable indoor world. "You're not going to migrate, are you?" Josh asked. "Winters around here aren't too bad."

"Chow time," Grock answered. "Chow time, dog dog."

"Josh. Josh, Josh, Josh! I wish you'd get it right, you wretched bird."

When Grock was sure there were no more cookies to be had, he went back to his box and turned his back, muttering in his own language.

"Rafferty's right, you know. You *are* weird."

In the garage, Josh hung his wet raincoat on a hook by the door and greeted Rafferty, who was attaching a light bulb to the cage of a new patient, a herring gull who stood inside, puffed and raggedy, its eyes closed, ignoring him. "It's just sick, I don't know what's wrong," Rafferty answered when Josh asked about it. "A guy found it in a supermarket parking lot and dropped it off this morning."

"Is there any medicine you can give it?"

"Probably not. Unless Pickett can tell what the problem is. Best thing to do is just keep it warm. We'll have to bring the electric heater out here soon. This place doesn't stay warm enough all winter."

Josh visited each of the occupied cages, saying good morning to the birds. Snow White had been moved to one of the large cages and no longer struck out with its beak when anyone came close. The gashes on its legs were beginning to heal. "Egrets go farther south for the winter, don't they?" he asked.

"Mostly they do. Why?"

"I was just wondering if Snow White would be well in time."

"In time? Listen, kid, it's not like a train leaving— one time only. When that bird's well, if the weather's too cold, it'll go looking for a place that's warmer. Otherwise, it'll stick around till the weather does get too cold. Changeable as it is around here in the fall, there's no telling."

Josh reached the cormorant's cage. He'd named the bird Henry, for no particular reason except that the name seemed to fit. He was particularly fond of Henry, as he was of Snow White, because they were the first birds he'd worked with. "How's it going this morning, Henry?" he asked as he bent to look into the cage. The bird was not standing as usual. He was a black huddle at the bottom of the cage.

"Rafferty!" Josh yelled. "Come here!"

"What's the matter?"

"Henry." It was all Josh could say.

Rafferty came and stood for a moment, looking into the cage. Then he opened the door and gently reached in to take out the still form of the cormorant. "We lost this time," he said.

Josh felt his eyes filling with tears. Henry had looked all right when Josh had said good-bye when he left last night. Now his eyes were glazed and empty, like the glass eyes of a bird in a museum. What had happened? And how? Josh felt sick. The bird looked almost the same as before. But so different! What was life anyway, that it could just snuff itself out like that between one night and the next morning? Between one minute and the next? "What'll you do with him?"

Rafferty put the body into a box—the same box they'd brought him in, Josh saw—and closed the flaps. "Take him to Pickett for an autopsy. Maybe he'll find out what killed him."

"Infection? From the hooks?"

"Could be. Or heart failure. We can't always tell." Rafferty took out the huge loose-leaf binder he kept his records in and entered Henry's death and the date.

"Pickett's report will go in here, too, if he has one. This record keeping is one of the jobs you can take over. It isn't my favorite. How's your handwriting?" Josh stood looking at the closed box. "Josh?"

"Sorry. My handwriting's lousy."

"Can't be much worse than mine. Or Pickett's, for that matter."

Josh looked at the other cages. Would those birds, too, turn into lifeless lumps of feathers in the dark? And would Rafferty expect him to record their deaths like that: "Found dead, so-and-so date, cause unknown"?

"Joshua; the odds aren't great. I told you that. You can't do this if you have to win every time, because you don't. Henry won't be the last we lose. If you save half the birds you get you're doing well. It's *those* you think about, not the losses. Each one you save is one more that would have died without you. Think about Grock. And Long John Silver. And Gainsborough."

It didn't help. Josh remembered the way Henry had stood so quietly, not striking out with that deadly hooked beak, trusting them to save him. And they'd let him down. Taking out the hooks hadn't been good enough. He thought about the fishermen whose hooks had killed the bird. Did they really care? How had they done it, anyway? A careless cast? Would they do it again, to another bird? Rafferty had said it was a big step forward, just convincing them to go to the trouble of bringing in birds instead of cutting the line and letting them go off to certain death. But Henry had died anyway, so what good did any of it do?

"What lives, dies," Rafferty said, his voice firm.

Josh rubbed a hand across his eyes and wiped the tears on his jeans. "It shouldn't be that way," he said. "It shouldn't." He could hear the childishness in his own voice. So what? He *was* a child. And death shouldn't be part of anything. It shouldn't be!

Rafferty closed the notebook and put it away. Then he put his hands on Josh's shoulders, gripping almost hard enough to hurt. "Take a break, Josh. I'll feed the birds. Come inside—I've got a book I've been meaning to give you to read. Might as well start now."

Rafferty pushed Josh ahead of him into the living room and sat him on the couch. He scanned the shelves a moment, then took down a book and handed it to Josh. "You know Durrell? Gerald Durrell?"

Josh shook his head. What did he want with a book now? How would a book change anything, make anything better?

"You should know his stuff. If anybody should, you should."

Josh looked at the book and shook his head again. "I don't feel like reading."

"Tough. That's your job for now. You want to work for me, you do what I tell you to do. Got that?"

"Okay," Josh said reluctantly. He didn't have much choice.

Rafferty left, and Josh sat on the couch, the book in his hand, staring at the rug. Rafferty's wife had died. She'd made that rug and she'd died, he thought. But Rafferty hadn't said how. Josh knew how his father had died—in a motorcycle accident. Did it make any difference *how* somebody died? Had Rafferty found his wife dead one morning the way they'd found Henry? Alive one minute, dead the next? And no reason? Or had there been an accident? And the dog, Rafferty's Doberman, had died, too. Not long ago. Did you get used to things dying? Was that why Rafferty could sit there and write in the notebook and not think about the cormorant that had trusted him? Josh remembered then that Rafferty had said dogs ought to live longer. And he remembered the way his voice had sounded when he'd said his wife had died. Maybe you didn't get used to it.

He looked down at the book he was holding. *My Family and Other Animals*. It might as well be school, he thought, being sent in here to read. Would Rafferty ask him questions about the book later? Give him a quiz? "What happened on page one hundred and three?" Josh sighed and opened the book. As the rain beat against the windows, he settled deeper into the couch and began to read.

"Lunch break," Rafferty said, and Josh looked up to see him standing in the doorway to the living room, drying his hands on a kitchen towel. "What do you think of the book?"

"You didn't tell me it was funny!"

"You didn't ask."

"It's true, isn't it?"

"Of course. It's autobiography."

"Gerald Durrell was a lot like me, then."

Rafferty raised his eyebrows. "He was? Think of that."

"I suppose that's why you wanted me to read it." Rafferty shrugged. "And he didn't go to school!"

"It occurred to me that might interest you."

"His mother got him a tutor, though."

"Mothers are like that." Rafferty snapped the towel at him. "Let's eat. You can take the book home if you want."

"I want. Were British families like that back then, or were the Durrells different?"

"I think it's safe to say they were different. I'm going to get the mail."

"I wish I could live on Corfu like he did!" Josh said, as Rafferty opened the front door.

"The Greek islands have changed since the thirties just like everything else. Anyway, Durrell didn't go there on his own, you know. He just made the best of where he found himself. Anybody can do that. Any time."

"Yeah, well, it would be easier in Corfu." Rafferty

went out and Josh headed for the kitchen to get his lunch. He poured himself a glass of milk and set out his sandwich and apple. Rafferty still hadn't come back in. He must have found something interesting in the mail for a change, Josh thought. Suddenly, Rafferty bellowed a curse Josh had never heard him use before. Moments later he stormed into the kitchen waving a sheet of paper, his face scarlet.

"I told you Tucker was a devious bastard!"

"What is it? What did he do?"

"He filed a grievance against me with the zoning commission. He told them I'm 'harboring livestock' in a residential zone. I've got thirty days to get rid of the birds. Thirty days!"

Josh watched Rafferty stomp across the kitchen and back again, the letter crumpled in his hand. "Can they do that?"

"Of course they can do that!" Rafferty slammed his fist down on the counter. "Of course they can."

"But isn't there anything *you* can do? Can't you explain—"

"I don't know what I can do. But if Tucker thinks I'm going to knuckle under without a fight, he's crazier than I thought."

That afternoon, while Josh cleaned cages, Rafferty remained in the house. Josh had the impression that he was mostly pacing and muttering to himself, though he heard him talking on the phone a couple of times. It was almost four when Josh returned to the garage after taking a pail of fish out to Gainsborough and found Rafferty digging through a drawer under the counter.

"I've got a plan," he said without looking up. "It could just work."

"What is it? Can I help?"

"We'll see. I'm going to apply for a variance."

"Variance?"

"A zoning variance. It allows one property in an area to be zoned differently from all the rest."

"Would that let you keep the birds?"

"If I can get it. Pickett says it won't be easy, since Tucker has already complained. But there's an organization that could help, the Neighborhood Association. The zoning commission has to hold an open hearing on any request for a variance, and anyone can go to the hearing to argue for or against it. This Neighborhood Association has a very good record for getting the commission to rule the way they want it to."

"And they'd go to the hearing and argue for you?"

Rafferty laughed a short, dry laugh. "They'd be more likely to argue against me."

"Why?"

"For one thing, I'm not exactly everybody's favorite neighbor. You may have noticed a slight lack of attention to the front lawn, for instance."

"Nobody cares about stuff like that."

"Don't kid yourself. The Neighborhood Association is in business to protect property values, and property values have a whole lot to do with how well people take care of their houses and yards—how the neighborhood looks and who lives here. Nobody wants to live next door to a dump."

"Your house isn't a dump."

"Let's just say it's no showplace. And I'm not universally loved. Like I said, I don't fit the uniform."

Josh frowned. "Then how can they help?"

"I have to convince them, that's all. And do it before Tucker gets wind of what I'm doing. If he hears about the variance, he'll try to get them on his side, I guarantee it. I have to persuade them that what I'm doing here is *good* for the neighborhood."

"That's obvious, isn't it?"

Rafferty shook his head. "For once, you sound like a ten-year-old."

"What does that mean?"

"Never mind. What I've got to do now is write one hell of a speech. Pickett suggests doing a slide show with it. I've got lots of slides in here somewhere. Neighborhood Association meetings are the last Tuesday of every month. That's this coming Tuesday. If I file for the variance first thing Monday morning and get the Neighborhood Association on my side Tuesday night, Tucker'll never know what hit him. Pickett knows the president of the association board, and he's going to get me on Tuesday's agenda. Next month would be too late."

Josh looked around the garage. Rafferty had to win!

What he was doing here was too important to be stopped. Snow White and Stanley and Richard the Second and the new gull—they were lives. Whole, separate lives. All those people with their backyards on the water surely had to be aware of the birds they saw every day. Surely they'd want someone taking care of them.

Rafferty held up a yellow box of slides. "Here they are. And I've got some others here someplace. Can you finish up in here while I start sorting these?"

"I'm nearly done now."

"Good."

"I can come over and help this weekend, too," Josh offered.

Rafferty grunted and opened another drawer. Josh put the empty bait bucket away and went to check on the sick gull. Rafferty trusted him, he thought. In spite of his being only ten. He'd shown him what to do for the birds and was letting him do it. By himself. After only a week. "You're one lucky bird," he whispered to the puffed-up gull. *And so am I*, he thought. A gust of wind blew rain against the windows above the cages. Josh looked at the box on the table and thought of Henry lying inside. He didn't want to think about Henry. Think about the winners, Rafferty had said. Think about the winners.

· 13 ·

B Y THE TIME Josh got home it was nearly dark, the first time he'd felt that winter was really closing in. The rain had stopped, but the wind, if anything, was colder. He took Nimbus for her walk, running a good part of the way to keep warm, Nimbus leaping and barking at his elbow. He wondered if Nimbus knew that winter was coming and whether she liked it. Her long, shaggy coat was better suited to the cold, of course, but he thought she probably liked her life in the summer, exploring with him in *Squeak*, better.

His mother was sitting at the kitchen table when he came in, a cup of tea in front of her. "Have you been sitting there all day while I've been working?" he asked.

"Naturally," she said. "Don't you know about housewives? Nothing but tea and soap operas all day."

Josh listened. "I've got news for you. That thing with no picture is a stereo, not a television. And that sounds like Mozart."

117

"Don't quibble over details. Sit!"

"Mind if I make myself some cocoa first? It's cold out there."

"Okay. But I've got something to tell you, so get on with it."

Josh lifted the teakettle. It was still hot and nearly full. "Won't take but a minute. And I've got something to tell you, too." He was hoping his mother and George would have some ideas about getting Rafferty's Neighborhood Association on their side.

"I've found you a school," his mother said.

Josh turned to look at her, noticing for the first time that she was not dressed in her usual jeans and sweat shirt. She was wearing a suit. And makeup. His chest felt suddenly tight. He couldn't seem to get his breath. "School?"

"Yes." Emily smiled a radiant smile and held up a brochure she'd been looking at. "You're going to love it, Joshie. Just love it!"

The kettle began to hiss, and he took it off the burner before it could whistle. School. The word was like a club against the back of his head.

"I went to visit this school today and had a conference with the principal."

"You didn't tell me you were going to do that," Josh said, forcing the words past whatever seemed to be blocking his throat.

"I didn't know whether I'd like it or not," his mother said, "so I didn't see any point in a big hassle."

Josh didn't answer. He stirred the water into his mug, scarcely aware of what he was doing.

"It's really different, Josh. Not at all like the Everett School. It has two art studios, a separate science lab, and a whole room full of computers!"

"Computers?"

"You'll have fun with computers. The principal says the computer lab's the most popular room in the school."

Josh sat across the table from his mother and patted Nimbus, who sat next to him and put her chin on his knee. Computers! What did computers know about sunlight glittering on the water, or the smell of the marsh, or the cry of a sea gull? He didn't think he would have fun with computers. His mother pushed the brochure across the table and he glanced at it dully. Didn't she understand? Didn't she see that he couldn't go back to school? Rafferty needed him, especially now. And what he was doing for Rafferty was important, in a way that having fun with computers, even if that were possible, could never be. He turned the pages of the brochure, barely seeing the smiling faces, the teachers pointing at blackboards or leaning over microscopes.

"All I want you to do, Josh, is go there and see what it's like. Get a sense of the atmosphere. It's so much more open, so much more relaxed than what you're used to, I'm sure you'll like it if you give it a chance."

"Do they teach long division?"

His mother frowned. "Long division? I suppose so. Schools do."

"So what's the difference?"

She sighed. "Trust me. This school *is* different. I've made arrangements for you to spend the day there on Monday."

"Monday?" With Rafferty having to be ready for that meeting the very next night? Rafferty would need him Monday more than ever. "I can't go Monday."

"You can't? Don't you mean you don't want to?"

Josh shook his head. "I mean I can't." His mother's face hardened. Obviously, he couldn't simply refuse. "Can I do it Wednesday instead? Rafferty needs me Monday. And Tuesday, too. It's really important, Mom, honest. Can't we change it to Wednesday?"

His mother gazed at him for a moment. "I wish I could understand what's happening with you, Josh. I really do. If I call and change it to Wednesday will you do me a favor in return?"

"What?"

"Keep an open mind."

At dinner Josh didn't get a chance to bring up Rafferty's zoning problem. His mother began talking about her visit to the school, but she didn't get very far either. George was worried about some money problems the university was having, and it was all he wanted to talk about. Josh didn't listen. The prospect of going back to school overwhelmed everything else.

It was as if he'd managed to escape one net, only to find himself heading toward another. Worse, he'd had a taste of freedom. He knew how life could be—how it was supposed to be. He couldn't give that up now. When the meal was over, he cleared the table, loaded the dishwasher, and told them he was going up to his room to read.

His mother handed him the school brochure. "Take a look at this, too, Joshie. And remember, an open mind."

And so he did. He lay on his bed, with Nimbus next to him, and turned the slick pages. The people looked happy enough. Of course. Why else would they use their pictures in a brochure designed like a magazine ad to sell the school? He read the section on the school's philosophy. *Individualism*, it said. *Attention to each student. Caring and dedication.* What else would they say? Didn't Dr. Ellsworthy use phrases like that? They were only words, after all. There was a page of rules, too. Josh couldn't see how the rules fit with "individualism." Rules were made by people like Tucker and the zoning commission. Rules were to keep lawns neatly mowed and men like Rafferty under control, and kids doing long division. *Rules and uniforms*, he thought. *Rules and uniforms.*

Josh was standing in the center of a huge field, a soccer ball at his feet. Around him he could hear yelling, and he knew he was supposed to kick the ball, but he couldn't remember which way he was supposed to be going. Suddenly he was aware of people coming at him—fast—from all sides. He'd have to kick the ball quickly or it would be too late and everybody would be mad at him. But he still didn't know which way. He tried to pull his foot back, but it was as if his shoe were made of concrete. He could hardly lift it. There were hands on his arms, then, and voices in his ears. He wanted to shout that people were cheating, that it was against the rules to touch a player, but no sound would come. He tried to kick again, dragging himself away from the hands, and his foot connected at last. He had kicked the ball, and now everyone would let go. Only they didn't. The hands only closed more tightly on his arms, hurting. He looked down at the place on the grass where the ball had been. But there was no ball. At his feet lay Cole Simms. It was Cole he had kicked—Cole, whose pale eyes looked up at him without expression. Fury overtook him and he kicked again. He wanted Cole to go away. The voices grew louder, and he kicked and kicked, his own eyes closed tightly. Finally he looked again and saw that Cole was gone. It was a bird on the ground in front of him now. A cormorant. "Rafferty!" he screamed. "Rafferty!"

Josh woke up panting. His sheet and blanket were stuck to his damp body, pinning him into his bed like a straitjacket. He struggled out from under them and pushed against Nimbus, who was lying on his legs. She didn't move. Josh reached for the battered monkey that he'd taken to bed with him as long as he could remember and lay in the dark, his eyes wide open, trying to will away the feeling of the dream. "It was only a dream," he whispered into the sparse plush of his monkey's head. "Only a dream. Nothing to be scared of."

When at last the terror of the dream had begun to fade, he knew he didn't want to go back to sleep. He dragged his feet away from Nimbus's weight and sat on the edge of his bed for a moment, the monkey in his lap. Finally, closing his eyes against the glare, he switched on his reading lamp. Nimbus shifted and woke up, blinking muzzily at him. "Go back to sleep," he told her. "I'm going to read." He picked up the Durrell book. He needed something funny. He also needed something to eat if he wanted to stay awake. "Stay here," he told Nimbus. "I'll bring you a biscuit when I come back." At the word "biscuit," she thumped her tail against the bed and started to get up. "No. I said stay."

The bare wood of his floor was cold. Outside he could see stars and a slice of moon. The wind had died down. Tomorrow would be another clear, crisp October day. Maybe good weather would bring good luck as the rain seemed to have brought bad. He slipped out into the dark hall and saw a line of light under his parents' bedroom door. When he was little, he used to crawl into bed with them when he'd had a bad dream.

Maybe now he could just go in and talk to them, tell them about the zoning commission. He started toward the door and heard his mother's angry voice. "That's not true! I'm thinking of Josh!" He couldn't hear George's answer, only the low sound of his voice. Josh crept closer to the door and leaned against the wall. His mother spoke again. "You know perfectly well why. Because he has his whole life ahead of him. How can he have a decent life without school? I don't like it either, but that's the way the whole society is set up, George. Besides, there's a law against it."

"I looked into that. The law's been tested here, and it didn't hold up. The judge ruled that parents could educate their children at home as long as they can show that they're learning."

"But he isn't! And he wasn't doing all that well in school."

"Of course he's learning. He'll get a lot out of working with Rafferty. Besides, he learns all the time all by himself. He probably knows more about the wildlife around here than anyone except a professional naturalist."

"What about spelling? And math? And writing a decent sentence?"

"All right, so maybe we have to do something about those things. But you said yourself he wasn't doing all that well in school. Shouldn't we ask why? You know perfectly well he's not dumb. In fact, he's extraordinarily bright! Maybe school methods aren't right for him. There must be better ways to teach him. One-on-one ways, maybe."

"This school is different. Let's at least see if their ways *are* better ways."

"Em, I don't want us fighting about this."

"Then don't fight."

"But I don't think we should force anything right now, either. That kid is really hurting!"

"Some things have to be forced. Anyway, hurting is part of life! He's my responsibility. He's only ten!"

That again. Josh tiptoed away from the door. She'd asked him to visit that school with an open mind. What good did it do for *him* to have an open mind if she didn't? It wasn't fair. What point was there in visiting the school if she was going to send him there no matter what he thought about it? It didn't matter how different the school was—there would be Matthew Whittakers there, and Cole Simmses. There would be rules and uniforms and people who didn't know a cormorant from a herring gull and wouldn't care. *And no time*.

He went back to his room, closed the door, and rummaged in the closet. Nimbus jumped off the bed, her tail circling. "You keep quiet," he whispered. He found his hiking boots and dressed quickly in jeans, a sweat shirt, and heavy socks. Then he turned out his light and, carrying his boots, slipped back out into the hall. Nimbus pushed past the door as he tried to close

125

her in, her claws clattering on the floor. Josh held his breath and listened. George and his mother were still talking. He put one hand on Nimbus's back and tiptoed carefully to the stairs. He had gone down only two steps when the light from under the door went out. He hurried the rest of the way down and out into the kitchen, stopping only long enough to take a few biscuits for Nimbus and some cookies for himself. Then he got his old winter jacket and a knit hat from the hall closet and let himself and Nimbus out through the patio door. "Now don't bark," he told her, as she began frisking around him. "If you do, I'll never take you out in *Squeak* again—*ever!*"

When he got down to the bulkhead with his life vest and the oars, he realized that he might not be taking Nimbus out in *Squeak* now, either. The tide was down and the boat was resting on the muddy sandbar below him. He stood for a while, looking across the water, so smooth now that the wind had dropped that he could see the reflection of the trees on the other side in the pale moonlight. It wasn't enough to stand here looking at the water. He wanted to be *on* it! He wanted to be out where the ducks spent the night, where the mullets were sleeping, or whatever passed for sleep with fish. He wanted to be out on the water with Nimbus where he wouldn't be anybody's responsibility but his own, and where his age didn't matter at all. He wanted to be just one more living thing in a vast world full of living things.

He put the oars down, slipped on his life vest, and untied the line. Then he climbed down next to the boat and coaxed Nimbus to jump into it. "Sit now," he ordered. "And hold still." He hauled the bow around toward the water, his feet sinking into the mud as he pulled. The odor of decay engulfed him, and he breathed through his mouth to keep it out. Carefully he moved back to the stern and found a rock that offered decent footing. He pushed until the front half of the boat was in the water, found another rock, and gave a final shove, leaping in at the last possible moment. He settled himself on the center seat and found that the stern was still on mud, so he used one of the oars as a pole to shove with. *Squeak* was floating. He fitted the oars into the oarlocks and began rowing.

He'd never been on the river at night before. It was much lighter than he'd have thought. Late crickets chirped steadily all around, and the ducks, whose silhouettes he could just make out at the far edge of the channel, muttered sleepily to each other. Every so often one quacked loudly in a complaining tone. No wonder they slept so much during the day, he thought, if they spent such restless nights.

Aside from the crickets and the ducks, everything was very still. Across the river most of the houses were dark; only streetlights showed through the trees. What Josh wanted to do was to row right down the river and into the bay and then out into the ocean and on. There would be an island somewhere, like the island of

Corfu, where Gerald Durrell had grown up free to wander with his dogs, to explore in his boat, to watch the animals and birds and insects he loved. *He'd* grown up all right! He wrote books now and had his own zoo especially for endangered species. He hadn't had to go to school to have a good life. And his life counted for something, made a real difference in the world—saved lives! *It's possible*, Josh thought, staring up at the stars as he rowed. *It has to be.* Then he just rowed, savoring the darkness and the quiet, trying not to think at all.

Not until he had pulled *Squeak* up next to the john-boat did he realize he'd been coming to Rafferty's.

· 14 ·

Josh knocked again, louder. Rafferty was almost
certainly asleep—the house was completely dark.
Behind him, Grock muttered and grumbled but didn't
come out of his box. Josh had just about decided
to give up and start for home again when the light over
the back door went on. The door opened a crack, then
flew back the rest of the way, showing Rafferty in an
old plaid bathrobe, his bony feet bare and white looking, his hair standing out at odd angles from his head.
"Joshua Taylor, what in the name of heaven are you
doing here at this hour?"

Josh shrugged. He didn't really know what he was
doing there.

"I suppose this is Nimbus." At the sound of her
name Nimbus started to jump up, but Rafferty caught
her in the chest with his knee and she sat down, looking up at him through the fringe of hair over her eyes.
"That's better." He ruffled her ears and she wiggled all

over, her tail circling double time. "Good girl." Rafferty looked pointedly at Josh's muddy boots and shook his head. "If you intend to come in, take those off first. What about her?"

"She didn't get into the mud," Josh assured him as he removed his boots.

When Josh was sitting, stocking-footed, at the kitchen table with Nimbus beside him, Rafferty leaned against the counter and ran his hand through his hair. "All right, kid. You've got ten minutes for an explanation, and then I go back to bed."

"I don't have one. I mean, I didn't really intend to come here. I started rowing, and here I am. I just needed to get away for a while."

"You have this urge to get away in the middle of the night very often?" Josh shook his head, and Rafferty sighed. "First thing you do is call your folks." Josh rubbed Nimbus's head and didn't answer. "Joshua, I said you have to call your folks. Or do you want me to?"

"It would only wake them up and get them upset over nothing," Josh said. "They don't know I'm gone."

"And suppose they happen to check on you and find your bed empty. Don't you suppose they'd be a little upset then?"

"They won't check on me now—they're sound asleep. And anyway, tomorrow's Saturday and they'll sleep late. They're never up before nine. I can call them in the morning . . ." he looked up hopefully, "if I can stay here till then."

"I don't know. . . ."

"Honest, they won't know I'm gone. They sleep like rocks. I can call them tomorrow, or I can leave early and be home before they're even up. No sense waking them up now."

"That's nice. I like that. Me, you wake up at two A.M., *them* you wouldn't want to bother."

"I'm sorry."

Rafferty pulled the belt of his robe tighter. "All right. But if they *do* notice you're gone, you'll have some heavy explaining to do. They'll want to know why I didn't take you right back home."

"It'll be okay," Josh said. "I'm sorry about waking you up."

"Mmmm. How's Nimbus at taking orders?"

Josh gave her the hand signal to lie down. She looked at him for a moment, as she always did, as if she were deciding whether to do it or not, then complied. "She's slow sometimes, but she usually does what I tell her."

"Good. I don't want her causing any trouble with the birds in the morning."

"I don't think she'd go after any of them. I usually take her out with me when I go exploring. She's outgrown chasing things."

"Dogs don't outgrow chasing," Rafferty said. "They

have to be trained out of it. You must have done a fair job with her."

"Thanks."

Rafferty crossed his arms in front of his chest. "All right, if I let you stay, I deserve to know why you felt this great urge to 'get away.'"

Josh stared at the front of the refrigerator. "Mom's sending me back to school," he said finally, his voice low.

"Not in the middle of the night, I presume."

"I heard her arguing with George about it, and I just left. She doesn't care whether I like the school or not, I just have to go there. I'm not going to have any choice."

"People don't always have choices."

Josh felt tears wanting to come, so he bent down and patted Nimbus. "I hate school!" he said.

"Lots of people hate school. But they have to go. It's pretty much the way things work."

"I'm not lots of people."

"No, you're not."

"Do you know what it's like? The stupid stuff they make you do? The time they take away from you for nothing—every single day?"

"It's probably not much different from when I was in school. Maybe a little worse."

"Much worse," Josh said. "Or else there's something wrong with me, because I can't stand it. I really can't!"

Rafferty pulled out the chair opposite Josh and sat down. "What's the difference between a human brain and a bird's, Josh?"

"What?" He blinked. "I don't know."

"Sure you do. What's the difference?"

"You mean thinking?"

"Do you know the constellations?"

"Some of them."

"How do you know them?"

"Well, I've read about them."

"Exactly. Some birds hatched last spring can fly thousands of miles this fall, guided by the stars, to the same place their species has been flying to for thousands of years. No books needed. They know the stars, period. The information they need is all there from the beginning. But if you worked with a bird for a hundred years you couldn't teach it to read. And if you tried to tell it the stories people have made up about the stars, the myths behind the constellations, the bird wouldn't understand a thing you said, much less could it make up stories of its own."

"So?"

"So how much choice do you think a bird has?"

"It doesn't need choice. It knows what it is."

"It has a bird's brain. You have a human brain, Joshua. It doesn't matter whether you like it or not. Whoever runs the universe doesn't ask permission. Yours is a reading, storytelling, learning brain, and

133

you're stuck with it. Which do you think is better? The brain with a chemical map of the stars built in? Or the one that turns stars into pictures and makes up stories about them?"

"I don't know."

"There are plenty of things human beings can't do. We can't smell what Nimbus smells or see what Grock sees. We can't hear whole sound frequencies or see whole bands of light. We can't swim blind like a dolphin or pick up electrical impulses through our skins like a shark. But we can change the world. Because we certainly can learn."

"You're standing up for school, too?" Josh felt betrayed. It was Rafferty who had given him the Durrell book.

"Of course not. If I'm 'standing up for' anything, as you say, it's the possibilities of your brain. What you do with it is up to you. Suppose they did send you back to school. Does that school have any control over what goes on inside your head?"

"I guess not."

"So, what you do with your brain is up to *you*. It is now and it always will be."

There was more to it than that, Josh thought. This wasn't just about learning or about control or about school methods. It was about not fitting. It was about the way Matthew Whittaker and the others treated Cole Simms—or anyone else who was different. About the way they didn't value living things or anything Josh thought was important. Josh wasn't one of them. If they were what kids were supposed to be, what humans were supposed to be, maybe there was something terribly wrong with him. Not even Rafferty could understand. "I'd rather be a bird," he said. "I don't make it as a human being, and I don't want to. I don't *like* the human brain!"

Rafferty stood up. "Enough of this. I've got too much to do this weekend to spend all night talking. You're going to bed so I can get some sleep. Come on. I'll get a sleeping bag."

Nimbus was standing in the bow of *Squeak* and talking to him, telling him where to row. His mother was sitting in the stern, holding a timer that was ticking loudly. He had to get somewhere before the timer went off, and he was rowing as hard as he could, but the boat didn't seem to be moving. The timer began to ring. He let go of the oars. He'd lost. The timer rang again and became the phone. He was in a sleeping bag on the couch in Rafferty's living room. Sunlight lay in patterns across Nimbus on the floor next to him. Rafferty was talking on the phone.

"I'll be there," he said. "What're the chances? . . . They still around anywhere? . . . Okay. See you in a few minutes."

He came into the living room, already dressed.

"That was Jackson at the pier. He's got a couple of wounded sea gulls. Kids with slingshots got them. I've got to go."

Josh started to get up. "I'll go with you."

"No, you won't. It's eight-thirty. You call your folks. Then, if they don't mind your staying awhile, get yourself something to eat and feed the birds."

Before Josh could unzip the sleeping bag, Rafferty had gone. Nimbus jumped onto the couch and Josh shoved her off. "Not on Rafferty's furniture," he told her. "He says a dog's place is on the floor." He stood up and stretched. "Come on. I'm hungry."

When he'd eaten a piece of toast, Josh gritted his teeth and called home. It was obvious when his mother answered that she'd been asleep. "Hi, Mom," he said, keeping his voice bright and casual. "Sorry I woke you. I came over to Rafferty's but forgot to leave you a note. Is it okay if I stay here for a while? He's got some work for me."

It was easy to get permission when she wasn't quite awake. He'd have to remember that, he thought as he hung up. She hadn't asked a single question. "Let's go, Nimbus. I want you to meet Grock."

When they went outside, the flock of mallards Rafferty fed every day flew up and over the water, their wings whistling. Nimbus looked in their direction and then began sniffing the ground. Grock flew out of the dogwood and landed on Josh's shoulder. "Hello," he said. "Get out!"

"Make up your mind," Josh said. "Grock, this is Nimbus. Nimbus, this is Grock."

Nimbus, busy at the base of the tree, looked up only briefly and went back to sniffing. "Chow time," Grock said, cocking his head at Josh. If a crow could smile, Josh thought, Grock would be smiling—that ingratiating smile he used so often himself. So much for introductions. Crow and dog ignored each other entirely. "Okay," he said. "Chow time for everybody."

Just then Nimbus caught sight of Gainsborough. She stood very still and the fur rose along her back. The heron stood equally still, glaring back at her. Nimbus took a step forward, and Gainsborough raised his huge wings. Slowly but smoothly, the dog turned and headed for the dock, looking for all the world as if she'd intended to go that way in the first place. Josh laughed. "Coward!"

"Bad dog!" Grock shrieked. Nimbus glanced back at them, put her tail between her legs and kept going. At the end of the dock she sat down and stared across the water. Clearly she wasn't going to bother the birds. Josh went to get Gainsborough's breakfast.

He had finished feeding the outdoor birds when he heard the truck in the driveway. He called Nimbus into the house and went out to where Rafferty was pulling a box out of the passenger side of the pickup. "How are they?" he asked.

"One was dead when I got there," he answered. "Get the door, would you?"

Josh held the garage door open while Rafferty maneuvered the box through and onto the counter. He left the box closed while he rummaged in the medicine cupboard. "How's this one?" Josh asked.

"Bad." Rafferty took a small blue-and-white box out of the cupboard, tipped a vial of clear liquid out, and tore the paper off a disposable syringe.

"What's that? Antibiotic?"

"No." Rafferty filled the syringe and then stood looking at the closed box. "You'd better go inside," he said finally.

"No! Why? I want to help."

"You heard me. Go in."

Josh didn't move. He looked at Rafferty's face, at the deeply etched lines, the mouth set and firm, and he understood. "That isn't medicine."

"No. Do what I told you."

"But you can't! You're supposed to *help* them."

"I am. Are you going in?"

"No."

"Suit yourself." Rafferty set down the syringe and carefully opened the flaps of the box.

Josh looked in and looked away, but it was too late not to have seen. Inside, a sea gull lay on its side, its black head a mass of blood, its eye missing. The wing was wrenched backward at an impossible angle, the gray feathers spattered with blood. Its side rose and fell as it breathed.

Rafferty picked up a clean white towel and tossed it

to Josh. "Here. You want to help, help. Hold him—gently."

"I—I can't pick him up," Josh said.

"Just put the towel over him and hold him still. He may not move anyway. It won't take long."

Josh did as he was told, holding the towel across the bird's body, pressing the cloth against the bottom of the box, afraid of hurting it more. He closed his eyes and turned his head, clenching his teeth until his jaws ached, forcing himself not to think about what was happening. It seemed forever before Rafferty spoke. "All right. You can let go now."

The gull looked no different except that the movement of its breathing had stopped. *"Larus atricilla,"* Josh said. "Laughing gull. It isn't laughing now!" He watched Rafferty close the box again, tucking the flaps in gently, as if the gull could still be hurt. "Slingshots?"

Rafferty nodded. "Slingshots."

"For which we can thank the human brain," Josh said. "That wonderful, reading, storytelling brain."

"We are what we are. Both sides of us."

"I don't understand. How could they do that?"

"They put out food and waited till the gulls came down to get it."

"I don't mean *that* how."

"I know. But I can't answer the other. You might as well know what goes on out there. I've seen worse. I'll see worse again."

139

"Well, I don't want to!"

"I didn't say I *wanted* to. I stated a fact. It's been said that we're the most vicious predators of all. Maybe we are, but there never was an eagle who built a refuge for rabbits, Joshua. Remember that."

Josh looked at the closed box and then at the bank of cages. "Eagles kill to eat. We just kill."

"Some of us. Only some of us. And we *aren't* the only ones. People who say we are want everything simple. It isn't. And there are all kinds of death. That gull could have died just as badly in a storm. It could have been blown into a building, or frozen to death, or starved this winter. Do you think it cared whether slingshots got it or cold? Or bacteria? Life isn't about the end. It's about everything else. Anyway, next spring when the ducklings hatch, there's one gull that won't be after them. Which would you choose, Josh? Gull or duck? Heron or fish?"

"Couldn't this bird have been saved?"

"One-eyed? Never able to fly again? Probably brain-damaged? What do you think?"

"I hate it!"

"Yes. Because you're you."

"Some comfort."

"I didn't mean it to be comforting."

Josh stayed the rest of the morning, taking care of the birds while Rafferty mowed the front lawn and sorted slides. The image of the mutilated gull kept reappearing like a double exposure in front of every bird, against every cage. It wasn't enough to get there after the damage had been done. As long as there were kids with slingshots, kids who could set fire to kittens, Matthew Whittakers who didn't know the difference between things that were alive and things that weren't, the battle would keep being lost. And none of those people would care. Only Josh would hurt. And Rafferty. Something was terribly wrong somewhere.

When Josh was ready to go home, Rafferty brought him a box of books. "Take these home with you," he said, "and do some research for me."

"Research?"

"I need some quotations to use in my speech. These guys say it a lot better than I can, and I could use their help."

"You want me to read all these? By Monday?"

"No, just skim them. What I need is something that makes connections—you know, about how saving wildlife is important to saving people. We can appeal to enlightened self-interest."

"How do I find stuff like that?"

"You'll get the hang of it as you go. Check the titles of essays or chapters. You'll find some that sound likely. Then just skim those."

"Okay," Josh said doubtfully.

"Don't just bring me the negatives, Joshua. We don't want to tell the association how rotten people are. The idea is to get them on our side, not turn them off. Pretend to be an optimist."

"Okay."

"You *can* come Monday, can't you? They're not sending you back to school yet?"

"No. I'm supposed to visit the new one Wednesday. They'll probably make me start Thursday."

"Don't be bitter, kid." Rafferty carried the box of books down to the dock and put them on *Squeak*'s stern seat. "Get home and get going on these. If anything can get that gull out of your head, they can."

As Josh and Nimbus rowed away from the dock, three crows flew over them, cawing loudly, and landed in the highest branches of the oak tree. Moments later they flew up again, still cawing, and Grock followed. Josh stopped rowing and watched as the four birds swooped up and down together and then flew off out of sight across the creek. Rafferty had said Grock flew with the wild crows sometimes. He hoped that was all he was doing. Josh wasn't sure he could stand it if Grock left. "Don't go," he said to the blank blue sky where the crows had been. "You haven't even learned to say my name yet!"

· 15 ·

MONDAY MORNING, as soon as George dropped him off, Josh hurried around to see if Grock had come back. He had. He was pecking in the gutter on the roof, throwing leaves and twigs down as he searched for edible tidbits. When he saw Josh he flew down to his shoulder. "You scared me to death," Josh scolded.

"Chow time," Grock said. "Bad dog."

Josh gave him the cookie he'd brought and went inside. "I got a few quotes," he told Rafferty, "but I don't know if they're what you want. I only managed to get through a couple of the books."

"Every little bit helps. I've got the slides chosen. Now I have to get them arranged properly. But first I have to get down to city hall and apply for that variance."

That afternoon the sick herring gull died. Josh recorded its death in the notebook as Rafferty asked him to, then went outside to visit Stanley. He'd been put in the pen with Gainsborough, his wing still bandaged. Lucky, the female mallard, had been freed from her cage, too, and had joined the other ducks. Josh couldn't be sure which one she was. She and Stanley were winners. Both winners.

Before taking him home, Rafferty showed him the slides and that, too, helped. The pictures showed clearly how Rafferty's operation had grown from the first two birds Dr. Pickett had asked him to keep to its present size, from makeshift wooden cages through the assembling of the intensive care unit. There were pictures of lots of winners—coots and ducks and gulls, egrets and herons and kingfishers, even a cormorant who looked exactly like Henry. There were baby birds Rafferty had raised when people who didn't know any better brought him what they thought were orphans. Best of all, Josh thought, were the before and after shots—birds with fish hooks or tangled in fishing line, birds with dangling wings or bloody wounds, followed by those same birds, standing on the dock ready to leave, or actually flying away. How could the Neighborhood Association possibly go against him after seeing those?

Tuesday was a perfect Indian summer day. The weather was a good omen, Josh decided, and only the first. The second came while he was throwing cracked corn to the mallards and Grock was sweeping back and forth, stealing bits from under their very bills. A sea gull landed with a shriek on the dock. Josh looked up and saw that it was standing on one leg. It shrieked again, then lifted itself into the air and flew to the pen, hovering for a moment before landing carefully next to the washtub, where it stood, peering into the water and uttering piercing screams.

"What're you doing back here, Long John, you old deadbeat?" Josh hurried to get a bucket of fish, hoping the gull's return didn't mean he wasn't making it on his own but glad to see him anyway, to know that he was still alive. He brought the fish out and tossed one into the tub. With a self-satisfied "Kweek," Long John snatched the fish and flew off with it. "You're welcome," Josh said, as he watched it disappear.

The third omen came later. Josh was cleaning the kingfisher's cage when Gainsborough suddenly raised his wings and half-jumped, half-flew over the pen's fence. Josh called Rafferty from the kitchen, and they stood together under the dogwood tree to watch. The heron stalked slowly toward the water, peering intently into the grass as he moved. When he reached the bulkhead, he stepped delicately onto a piling and stood there for a moment, his neck stretched upward, looking very tall. Suddenly he launched himself out over the water, his huge wings nearly brushing the surface, and flew heavily away, gaining altitude slowly and circling once before heading downstream toward the river.

Rafferty stood looking after him and his face seemed to change, all the lines and creases softening. One of the naturalists Josh had read over the weekend said that people had lost the capacity for joy. The naturalist was wrong, Josh decided.

"Well," Rafferty said at last. "Back to it. My speech is going to have to be terrific if we're going to be able to watch that around here again. Did I tell you the Game and Fisheries Commission is sending a man down from Richmond to support me at the meeting tonight?"

"Three times."

"Oh, yeah. Good."

Later, Rafferty called Josh inside to listen to his completed speech. He was planning to drop Josh at home, then go to Dr. Pickett's for dinner before the meeting, so he was dressed and ready to go. It was the first time Josh had seen him in a suit. He didn't look like himself at all, except his face, of course. There was no disguising a face that spent most of its life outside. Otherwise, he could be anyone, a retired banker, a lawyer, a school principal even. "How do I look? Like an upright citizen? Like a man who can be counted on to keep his trim painted and his grass mowed?"

"Nice uniform," Josh said.

"Very funny. There's a place even for uniforms, Joshua, and we can't afford to forget it. We have to live in the world, kid, if we're going to do anything about it."

"Okay. You look fine. But nervous."

"Don't be silly. Why would I be nervous? What do I have to lose? Except this." He nodded toward the back door. "And them. Not much as the world goes."

"Maybe not as the world goes, but for them, it's *everything*."

"Exactly. Now sit and listen to my speech. I'm using three of your quotations, so you're at least partly responsible."

Before the speech was finished the phone rang. Rafferty, cursing, went to answer it. As he talked, Josh thought about the meeting. They'd have to side with Rafferty, omens or no omens, because Rafferty was right and Tucker was wrong, and that's all there was to it. The slides and the speech made it clear. Besides, Dr. Pickett would be there, and the man from Richmond. Only an idiot like Tucker could take a stand against them. The association couldn't possibly be made up of nothing but Tuckers.

". . . completely?" Rafferty was shaking his head. "How'd it happen?"

Josh recognized a rescue call. What was it this time?

"Under the bridge? . . . Must have been. . . . Okay, thanks."

Rafferty hung up and came back to the slide projector. "Now, where was I?"

"What was that about?"

"A great blue," Rafferty said. "I'll go back one slide and get a running start."

"What about the great blue? What happened?"

"Hit by a car."

Josh thought of Gainsborough flying off. "It couldn't be Gainsborough?"

Rafferty shook his head. "Not a chance. He'll stay pretty close for a while. This happened clear down by Johns Creek."

"Well? Aren't we going to get it?"

"No."

"Why not?"

Rafferty ran a hand through his hair. "It lost a wing. Traumatic amputation."

"It's alive, though, isn't it?"

"It was when Smitty saw it. It fell onto an island under the bridge."

"Well, if it's alive, we have to get it!"

"Don't you ever listen? I don't try to save a bird that will never be able to live on its own. I'll be lucky to keep this place as it is. I can't turn it into a zoo."

"So you're just letting it die out there?"

"I'm not 'letting it die.' I'm just not going to try to save it. God, or the laws of nature, or whatever will let it die."

"We could save it. I'd keep it."

"Don't be silly. It's not a dog that you can give a bowl of Purina to once a day. It's a wild bird. A dangerous one at that. Anyway, it would be against the law. Besides, we probably couldn't save it. If it collided with a car hard enough to lose a wing, it'll have other injuries. It might have bled to death by now for all we know."

"We could at least find out."

"What we will do is leave it where it is, to die as quietly as the laws it lives by will allow. We'd only add to its pain by trying to capture it. Furthermore, even if I thought there *was* a chance, I couldn't do anything tonight. This speech is more important than any single bird. I'm fighting to keep this place for all of them."

"Just like nature," Josh said. " 'So careful of the type, so careless of the single life.' "

"That's an excellent quotation, Josh, because it's true. That's how it works. I didn't invent it."

"Then why save any of them? Why not just let nature work? Let them all die."

"Because I'm part of nature, too. And *my* nature makes me want to save them. As you so readily point out, human beings do more than their fair share of damage. I just do what I can in favor of balance. I can't save the world. I can't even try."

The sun had begun to go down, and the living room was heavy with shadows. "Come on," Rafferty said, straightening his tie. "I'll take you home and give the speech for Pickett. You've heard most of it anyway."

"Wish me luck," Rafferty said, as Josh got out of the truck. Josh watched him back out of the driveway.

"Luck," he said quietly. He hadn't shouted it. Rafferty probably wouldn't have heard anyway. Of course he wished him luck. Surely Rafferty knew that. But for some reason, he didn't feel like yelling it out right now. Not with a heron out there somewhere, dying.

Nimbus was barking in the house as Josh started around toward the back door. Next to the garage he stopped. An idea was beginning to take shape at the edges of his mind. If he didn't go inside right away Nimbus would stop barking, and his mother and George wouldn't know she'd been barking at him. It was nearly dark. They would be in the kitchen, getting supper. The light would be on. Dark outside and light in. If he didn't get too close to the windows, they wouldn't see him.

As quietly as he could, Josh crept into the garage and got his life vest, the oars, and his biggest net. He found a flashlight on George's workbench and tried the beam. It seemed bright enough. A light in their eyes paralyzed them, Rafferty had said. He wished he had his hat and gloves. It was getting cold. But those were inside; he'd just have to do without.

Staying far away from the kitchen windows, he made two trips down to the bulkhead, putting everything into the boat. He didn't begin to breathe normally until he was well out into the channel. They hadn't seen him.

Johns Creek, Rafferty had said. That was downstream, he knew, the opposite direction from Rafferty's, and not close. If they'd gone together, they'd have used Rafferty's johnboat and motor and been there fairly quickly. Rowing would take a long time. Josh shivered as drops of cold water hit the back of his neck. The wind was stronger than he'd thought, and the water was choppy. Spray hit him each time *Squeak*'s bow struck a wave. At least, he thought, the wind would be with him on the way back, when he'd have the bird to contend with, too. He hoped the net he'd brought was big enough. It would have to be. When he got home, he could get a box. There were some huge packing boxes in the attic. He refused to think about the possibility that the heron might already be dead.

He rowed on and on, straining against the oars, pushing *Squeak* against the wind and the waves, trying to ignore the cold. He thought of the bird. Compared to what it was suffering now, he was comfortable. He passed under two bridges, refusing to let himself be panicked by the darkness underneath or the roar of cars overhead. He was nearly there, he thought at last. Johns Creek was the next one. A huge house stood on the point where the creek met the river, its lawns manicured and floodlit, a dock reaching far into the river. A cabin cruiser was tied to the dock. Josh rowed past it, grateful for the light from the floodlamps and the shelter from the wind.

The creek, far narrower than the river, was far shallower, too, Josh realized. His oars had dug into the mud on the last sweep, sending up the rank, dead-fish-and-rotting-vegetation smell of the tideflats. He skimmed the oars along the water, and *Squeak* moved. So far so good. He hoped this wasn't one of the creeks that turned completely to mud at low tide. *Squeak* didn't need much water, but he couldn't row her on mud.

It was very dark as he moved up the creek. Trees made a barrier between the water and the houses. Crickets were still chirping, in spite of the chill, but less exuberantly than last Friday. Autumn was the end for them, Josh thought. No Rafferty on earth could save crickets from the winter. It wasn't part of the plan, as Rafferty would say. *What lives, dies.*

Josh heard a car and turned. The bridge was just ahead. He picked up the flashlight and shone it forward, where it caught a stand of reeds on the other side of the bridge. Maybe technically an island, he thought, but an awfully little one, not much more than a hummock of weeds. He clicked the light off and went back to rowing. Just as *Squeak*'s bow slid under the shadow of the bridge, she stopped. Josh dug in with the oars, and the smell of the mud rose ever stronger. The smell had been growing in intensity ever since he'd entered the creek. So it *was* a mud flat at low tide. And he didn't know where he was in the tide cycle. If it had been low in the middle of the night on Friday, what did that mean about Tuesday?

If he couldn't get back out to the river, there was no point in trying to get to the heron now anyway. He pushed the button on his watch to light it. Nearly seven o'clock already. How had it taken him so long to get here? Rafferty's meeting would be starting soon. "Luck," he whispered. "Good luck!"

He clicked the flashlight back on and played the beam over the underside of the bridge. Spray-painted graffiti were everywhere—swearwords, initials, dates, and two confederate flags. The human brain again, he thought. Wonderful.

As the light swept down the concrete stanchion to the surface of the creek, Josh grinned. The concrete was dry all the way to water. The tide had to be coming in. If it were going out, the concrete would be wet, at least just above the waterline. All he had to do was wait until it came up far enough to let him get *Squeak* as far as the island. Josh turned off the light and shipped the oars. He would go on as soon as he was floating again.

Twice *Squeak* floated free of the mud and he rowed closer to the tiny island, only to ground her again. Gnats flew up as he got closer to the reeds. He turned his collar up and hunched into his jacket, trying to ignore them.

Finally, the third time *Squeak* floated off the mud,

153

he was able to get her bow in among the reeds before she ran aground. He stood up, balancing himself as the boat tipped sideways, and looked at the island in the light of his flashlight. It was bigger than he'd thought, but a good part of it would be under water at high tide. Wishing he had on his boots, he stepped out of the boat. His sneakers sank into the ooze at the base of the reeds, and gnats clouded around his face.

He took the net and the flashlight out of the boat and then remembered what Rafferty had told him the day he'd first seen the egret—a bird will stay calmer if you keep it in the dark. If he got the heron paralyzed with the flashlight long enough to get the net over it, he should have something to cover its head. Why hadn't he thought to bring something to wrap it in? His jacket was all he had. He unzipped his life vest and dropped it. Then he shouldered the net, aimed the flashlight ahead, and started around the edge of the island, stepping carefully, partly to avoid sinking too deeply into the mud, partly to avoid frightening the heron, wherever it was.

He saw where it had been before he saw the bird itself. Near the water the reeds were broken and bent in an uneven circle. The light picked up a few feathers and glinted off a smashed beer can, next to a darkness on the flattened reeds that was probably blood. "It could have bled to death," Rafferty had said.

Josh had just about given up hope that he would

find the bird alive when his light was reflected in the heron's bright eye. The bird was crouched low, its one wing spread out to balance it, its head pulled into its shoulders. Where the other wing should have been there was nothing but dried blood and broken feathers and the white of bone. Josh felt a burning in his throat and swallowed hard. He would have to be as immovable as Rafferty if he were going to do this. He stepped toward it, keeping the light pointed toward its eyes. But the paralysis Rafferty had promised wasn't happening. Perhaps the light wasn't strong enough. The bird turned its head away and flapped its good wing vainly, its body heaving, its neck stretched out. Josh stepped back. What could he do if he couldn't get near enough to net it? He didn't want it to injure the other wing trying to get away from him. "I only want to help," he said to it, keeping his voice low and gentle. "I won't hurt you."

The bird turned and glared into the light, its eyes the same as Gainsborough's. In fact, Josh thought, this could be Gainsborough, except for the horror of that missing wing. He tried to move the net, to get it into position so that he could take a few steps toward the bird and swing the net quickly enough to stop it before it thrashed away. But the bird began flailing its wing again, and he realized he had moved the flashlight. Rafferty had said it was better with two people.

Maybe the thing to do was to back off for a minute,

get his jacket off, and try throwing that over the bird's head. At least the jacket had nothing as hard as the rim of the net to hurt the bird further. He set the flashlight and net on the ground and took his jacket off. Then, training the light beam directly at the golden iris of the heron's eye again, he took two careful steps. The heron didn't move. Josh held the jacket by the collar like a bullfighter's cape. "Easy. Easy," he whispered, moving closer. "I'm not going to hurt you," he repeated, knowing that he was almost certainly lying. How could he avoid hurting it, with that bone sticking out like that? He took a deep breath, tested the weight and balance of the jacket, and then threw.

"Wa-a-a-atch!" the heron rasped as the jacket fell on it, missing the head and falling across the body, hiding the jutting bone and dried blood. The bird flailed its wing again and struggled to get up, beating down the reeds around it. "Wa-a-a-atch!" The jacket slid off and lay in the mud. Josh tried to hold the flashlight steady. Now he would have to get his jacket back and try again—except that every time he tried to get close enough to reach the jacket, the bird began struggling. Where the wing had been, Josh saw the gleam of fresh blood. The wound had broken open and it was oozing steadily, the thick blood moving down across the blue-gray feathers. Josh gritted his teeth and lunged for the jacket, dropping the flashlight. As his fingers closed over the fabric, the bird struck, its beak tearing into the skin of his cheek, missing his eye by no more than a fraction of an inch. Pain flashed down his cheek and he jerked back, pulling the jacket away and dragging himself out of range. He put one hand to his cheek.

An eye for an eye, he thought. Blood was running down his cheek and dripping warmly onto his neck. He picked up the flashlight and shone it on his hand, red and sticky with blood. He had nothing to use for a bandage—his jacket was too dirty. He turned the beam of light toward the heron again. It had fallen back and was struggling to right itself. Then Josh saw its legs. They were broken. No wonder it had been crouched so low—the bird that had spent its life looking proudly down on the world. Had its legs been broken when the car hit it, or had that happened when it had fallen onto this wretched little hummock? What difference did it make? Rafferty had been right. Nothing he could do could save this bird, and all he had done was to terrify it, to add to its pain!

The burning sensation in his throat couldn't be swallowed down this time. He leaned away from the heron, his stomach heaving. In his mouth the burning, sour taste mingled with the taste of blood. The heron's beak had gone clear through his cheek. Josh spit and spit again, then took off his shirt and pressed it to his cheek.

The heron had managed to get itself upright again, and its head was hunched into its shoulders as it had been when he saw it first. The eye turned toward the light was bright. Cold. Somehow utterly clear. Without a human brain, it knew the rules far better than Josh. He thought of the little bottle of clear liquid and wished Rafferty were here with it now. He had made a mistake and there was no way to make up for it. "I'm sorry," he said. "I'm sorry." The bird didn't move. Its implacable eye stared at him—through him.

Josh took his jacket, the flashlight, and the net, holding his shirt against his cheek with his shoulder, and went back to *Squeak*. He was glad of the pain in his face, as if it could balance something. The heron had continued to fight, no matter how inevitable its death. Maybe that was one of the rules, too.

· 16 ·

IT WAS the rowing dream again, only colder. Nimbus must have pulled his covers off, Josh thought, and the cold was making him dream this way. If he could only open his eyes, he'd find himself at home in bed. Except that his eyes *were* open. And his hands were on the oars. The cold was real, a wind that came through the shirt he'd had to put on again, though it was sticky with blood. At his feet, his jacket lay in the bottom of the boat, too wet and muddy to do any good. And his life vest was gone—left on the island. He was breaking his mother's rule. This was a night for breaking rules, he thought, and could have laughed except that he hurt too badly to laugh.

The river seemed to be getting longer as he rowed. In spite of the following wind, in spite of the tide moving with him, he seemed to be getting nowhere. The lights along the shore all looked the same. He knew the only way to wake up from this dream that wasn't a dream was to get home, so he had to keep rowing. *In, pull, out, back.* The cold coming through his cheek was terrifying, but it helped him to keep going. *In, pull, out, back.*

He wondered if the meeting were over by now and if Rafferty had convinced them to help him with the zoning commission. Rafferty wouldn't want him working anymore after what he'd done tonight, but the work had to go on. The heron on that island would die, probably before morning. Other birds would die, as Henry and the new sea gull had. But Rafferty had to be allowed to save the ones he could! Whatever the force was that laid down the real rules, it had to be on Rafferty's side.

When he heard Nimbus barking, he could hardly believe it. He'd almost forgotten there would be an end to this ordeal. He tried to row harder, to cover the last of the distance more quickly, but there was no energy left. It was all he could manage to keep his arms moving. *In, pull, out, back.* When at last *Squeak*'s bow cracked into the bulkhead, he looked around and blinked into the light of a flashlight. His hands seemed frozen to the oars, and he couldn't let go, couldn't push himself up from the seat. He was too tired.

He was aware of voices then and felt himself being lifted and hauled up over the bulkhead, his legs scraping over the wood. Everything hurt. George set him down on the grass but kept an arm around him, supporting him as he swayed and nearly fell. Rafferty was there, he saw, and Dr. Pickett, who was holding Nimbus by the collar as she tried to get to him. His mother was crying. He was home.

Dr. Pickett had called the hospital before cleaning Josh's cheek. "You'll need a fancier stitcher than I am to close that up," he'd said. "But I'm afraid even Betsy Ross would leave a scar. I'll just get it cleaned and held together and then you can get over to the emergency room."

Josh was sitting on the counter next to the sink now, Nimbus at his feet, gazing up at him. "Did you win?" Josh managed to ask Rafferty before Dr. Pickett started working on his cheek and the burning and pain took over.

"Not yet," Rafferty said. "There's still the zoning commission."

"That's the least of your worries," the veterinarian said. "He got that bunch of people so excited tonight they wanted to take him on as a community action project—set up a foundation and give the place a name."

"That's all I'd need. I'd have to buy Tucker out to have room."

So something was on Rafferty's side, Josh thought. He looked at his mother, who was watching Dr. Pickett work, her hand pressed to her mouth. She hadn't yelled at him yet. No one had. He'd started to tell them what had happened, but they'd stopped him. When Rafferty had arrived to share the good news and learned that Josh had never come into the house, he'd known immediately where Josh had gone. So they hadn't needed an explanation for his cheek. Rafferty'd been just about to go home for his boat and come out after him when Nimbus started barking. No one had even told him how stupid it had been to go alone, to try to do what Rafferty had known could not be done. But it would come, he was sure. After they'd taken him to the hospital, after his cheek had been sewn up, it would come. Tomorrow was Wednesday and he was supposed to visit that school. He wouldn't be able to go.

"The school . . ." he started to say, in spite of the pain, but Dr. Pickett told him to keep quiet and let him work.

"Never mind that now," his mother said. "There's no hurry." He could only look at her. "I've been bullied, coerced, shamed, and scolded," she said. "They ganged up on me."

"You're dealing with gentlemen, Emily. We wouldn't do such things." Rafferty winked at George, and George put his arm around his wife.

"They seem to think there is room in the world for choice, Joshie," she said.

"More than one way to skin a cat," said Dr. Pickett, "if you'll excuse the expression."

"But . . ." Josh said.

162

"Hush. I'm almost finished here. Just a butterfly bandage now, and your folks can take you over to General."

"And then home to bed," his mother said. "And a good long rest."

"Not too long. We're going to have more work than ever, now that so many people know what we're doing."

Rafferty had said "we." Josh could hardly believe it.

"Don't think I've given up completely," his mother warned. "You have to at least visit that school and see for yourself. But if you hate it—well . . ."

"There *are* other ways, Josh," George said. "If that school doesn't work out, we can look for a tutor. And maybe it's just that school is a problem right now. Maybe later it'll be better."

"Gerald Durrell eventually went to school, you know," Rafferty said. "The British equivalent of high school."

George took his car keys out of his pocket. "I'll go get the car started, Em. Find him something warm to put on and we'll get going."

Dr. Pickett patted Josh on the back. "That's all I can do. They'll give you something for the pain when you get to the hospital."

"Okay. I'm sorry," Josh said to Rafferty.

"I know."

"The heron—"

"Don't think about it right now."

"What good is my brain if it can make mistakes like that?"

"Everybody makes mistakes. Your brain's ten and mine's sixty-eight. They *both* have a lot to learn. But they do learn, kid."

Emily brought a sweat-shirt jacket. "It's mine—a little big—but it'll have to do." She put the jacket around Josh's shoulders while Dr. Pickett packed his bag.

Rafferty lifted Josh down from the counter and guided him toward the door. The grip of his hands on Josh's shoulders was comforting. Josh wondered if the birds felt like this when Rafferty found them, if they knew those hands could make a difference.

"Wait," Josh said, when he was settled in the back-seat of the car. Rafferty stood where he was, holding the door open. "Did the heron know what was happening to it?" Josh asked.

"That it would die? I don't know. Not the way you knew."

"I hurt it."

"And it hurt you."

"It was defending itself—doing what it had to do."

"So were you. You thought it needed you. You were wrong, that's all. That's not so bad, Joshua."

George started the car and Rafferty stood back.

"You're part of it, kid, just like the rest of us. You're human, and you're supposed to be. You just have to have time to find out where you fit."

For the first time, Josh felt his eyes filling with tears. He hadn't cried about the pain, why now? Rafferty patted his shoulder and shut the door.

As George backed the car down the driveway, the lights of Rafferty's pickup truck blinked on. Josh waved as they passed it, and Rafferty waved back.

Josh leaned back against the seat, shutting his eyes against the tears, against the pain.

"I'm sorry you're going to have a scar," his mother said. "Does it hurt a lot?"

"Not too much." Against his eyelids, Josh saw again the heron's bright, unblinking eye. "I'll live," he said.